TIMOTHY

MARK TUFO

Copyright © 2012 by Mark Tufo
Copyright © 2012 by Severed Press
www.severedpress.com
All rights reserved. No part of this book may be reproduced or transmitted in any form or by any electronic or mechanical means, including photocopying, recording or by any information and retrieval system, without the written permission of the publisher and author, except where permitted by law.
This novel is a work of fiction. Names, characters, places and incidents are the product of the author's imagination, or are used fictitiously. Any resemblance to actual events, locales or persons, living or dead, is purely coincidental.
ISBN: 978-0-9872400-2-6
All rights reserved.

As always to my wife, my muse who more than once while proof reading this story turned to me and asked 'What's wrong with you?'

To the brave men and women of the armed forces, a thank you to each and every one of you.

TIMOTHY

It was a weekend day, Saturday to be specific, just like most. It was spent among twenty three screaming, crying, fighting, bratty six year olds, and did I tell you I don't much like kids? My secondary job as Spangle the clown was something I did on the side to pay my bills. My day job, which I have been encouraged by many a parent at said side gigs to not quit, was not making my ends meet. To be honest, my ends couldn't currently even see each other.

Why I chose to live in an upscale apartment in downtown San Francisco I'll never know. Wait, scratch that, I do know, it's for the chicks. If you live in the Asbury-Haight district you *have* to be loaded and nothing attracts a gold digger quite like gold. As a mid-level accountant at a finance firm during the week and a kid-detesting clown on the weekends I lived on a steady diet of Ramen Top Noodles and grilled cheese, most times without the cheese. I was, and I stress *was*, a man living way beyond my means but it all seemed worth it when I was in bed with yet another nameless beauty who was low on self esteem and high on ecstasy.

The day was cold and dreary even by San Francisco standards I had gone outside to get away from the claustrophobic cacophony that was spoiled children pent up indoors all hopped up on sugar and soda. Damn near lethal combination, if you ask me because I wanted to kill them. Alright not literally, at least not until a juiced-up Johnny bit me on my calf—the little fucker actually drew blood. And then his bitch mother had the audacity to yell at me when I hurled the little kid across the room.

"What is wrong with you?" she screamed, her finger in my face.

Just some background, I am six foot five inches tall and close to three hundred pounds. I played college football a few years back and was good enough to start, but I didn't have allusions of going pro. I just knew the NFL would have been a stretch and I didn't want to work that particularly hard for it. Kind of pathetic, I know; guys with five times my heart would have killed for my size. I took it for granted, I have been bigger than most for almost my entire life. Everything and I mean everything once I was seen by a coach was handed to me. My first coach gave me a bike just to join his team, and the perks got bigger and better as I started to cruise control through life. Sure with the size I possessed I had a fair number of pro scouts come and see my games; by then, though, I had moved on to my true passion, women, or more accurately, one night stands. Pursue, conquest, disposal—that was my creed, football was merely a means to that end.

I'm not sure why I didn't put it together that to move on to the next level would have ensured a steady supply of what I desired most, pussy. As an offensive lineman it wasn't my job to think, maybe that's a cop-out but I've never really stopped to think about it until now. Actually, was given the shitty accountant job which I was wholly unqualified for by a UCLA alum that was a season ticket holder and had appreciated the effort that I had put forth in ensuring that the Golden Bears won the BCS title that year. I could tell, Victor, my boss was beginning to regret his decision to ever hire me. He had to lay out a fair amount of cash for all of my custom built office furniture to accommodate my size, I even had an oversized calculator which for some reason still gave me inaccurate figures.

But back to my immediate predicament.

"You fucking goon!" The diminutive mom screamed as she kept poking her finger into my chest.

"Listen, Lady!" I yelled at her. "You're little fucking angel just bit me hard enough to draw blood," I raised my calf so that she could see the crimson circle that welled up on my Golden parachute pants. "And if you keep poking me in the chest I am going to return the favor in spades!" I had scared the shit out of men nearly the same size as me, this little rotund out of shape, ball of bitch was nearly shaking in her shoes, which were almost as ugly as mine and you have to remember I was dressed as a clown. She backed up a few steps and clutched her now sobbing snot-faced kid to her chest.

Twenty-two kids and about half that number of adults had all completely stopped what they were doing to watch the drama unfold. The little red-headed number that had hired me for the job was the first to act. Like a fool, I had taken it for almost half my normal rate thinking that I might get to check out if what she wore on top matched down below or even better had nothing to compare against at all. She was close to fifteen years my senior and was married with her own little brood of brats, but that had not stopped me in the past.

"I think that you should leave, Mr. Spangles," she said timidly.

"It's just Spangles," I fairly growled at her. "And I'm not going anywhere until I get paid."

I watched as she eyed the phone on the counter and then did the mental calculations of how much damage I could wrought before the police took their customary fifteen minutes to show up for an emergency. I have a temper, I know this and I used to use up all my anger on the field. Since my days of collegiate play were over I had learned differing ways to diffuse this anger, but between the kid biting me, his fat slob of a mother poking me in the chest, and the unsettling feeling that I was getting sick just all combined in me to make a caustic stew of malcontent. If Red was stupid enough to call the police, by the time they got here I don't think there'd be many people left standing to give a statement, women and children included. Especially the children.

Red paid me double my going rate, said she was concerned or some shit about my bite getting infected and that I should get it checked out. The fear that exuded off of her as she fished around in her purse, I've got to admit was exhilarating, if I didn't think that the police might now be on their way I would have taken her right there and then.

As it was I made sure to press my hard on up against her back as she escorted me to the door. Bitch damn near passed out when she felt the size of it.

"You don't know what you're missing," I said softly to her.

"You need to go," she answered me, shivering.

I did not look back as I got into my old Ford F-350, another 'gift' for choosing to go to UCLA. It was starting to show signs of age, but it accommodated my size and the shitty hundred fifty dollars I made today was not going to be enough to buy a newer one. I don't know what happened to Red after that day but I regretted not getting a go with her.

My head was splitting by the time I was around halfway home, so much so that I didn't pull over into my customary gas station and change, a la Superman. I did not want my neighbors to know that I moonlit as a clown, it would break the illusion that I was attempting to foster, the image of a successful business man, not many CEOs in waiting wore a bright red nose. The pressure in my sinuses was threatening to rupture through my face, the thought of stopping for an extra twenty minutes to change was incomprehensible. I needed to swallow an Oxycodone and three shots of Jack before this head fuck blossomed into a meltdown. I had once suffered a concussion from a late hit by one of the guys on our practice squad, that pain although excruciating was nothing compared to the daggers being thrust into my skull right now. The following week I had ended any hopes Pat Ryan had of making the starting team, I had clipped his knee, shattering his patella. "So sorry," I had said as I tapped the side of his helmet and got off of his tortured form. I don't think he heard me over his ragged screams.

I lived on the first floor not because I liked to listen to the douche bags above me walking around at three AM but because the rent was thirty-five dollars a month cheaper. So it was easy to see the little number that was on the lawn out front peeking through my windows as I rolled up.

"Fuck," I muttered, even that softly it reverberated through my jawbone and pitched the pain level just that much higher, and still I didn't learn my lesson as I asked myself what was she doing here. She knew the rules—I pick her up after a series of lies, we head back to my place for some wild anonymous sex. I then lie once more, telling her that I'll call her and then immediately throw her number out. I used to hang on to the numbers kind of like trophies but once in a moment of weakness I had called a girl back, we had gone on an actual date. It was awkward, we had tried to have conversations, and I discovered I wasn't nearly as smooth a liar if we both weren't liquored up. I had ended up dropping close to 200 bucks for the night and I hadn't even gotten laid, she said that she had wanted to get to know me better. I had told her that she'd already met my penis and it was a little late for the rest.

My skull was splintering, I knew for sure that it was. And if I remembered correctly Marie-Barbie-Twat had a high-pitched nasally laugh. Her orgasm had sounded like a seal being clubbed to death, slowly. Almost made me lose my hard-on.

Maybe she won't notice me, I thought wrongly. Pretty tough to miss a three hundred pound man, especially when he's dressed up brighter than a rainbow. At least the size twenty-seven shoes were off, pretty tough to drive with them on.

"Timothy?" She whined as I got out of my truck.

I covered my face with my hand hoping to block out the sun and her voice.

"I thought you were a pilot? My girlfriend told me you were full of shit, she said you were too big to be a pilot. I can't believe I fucked Bozo," she nearly shrieked.

Fucking daggers, her talking was like a samurai sword sawing through my head. With my free hand I wrapped it around her face and pushed her away, she just barely caught her balance or she would have landed on her spectacular ass, even in this amount of pain I would have still enjoyed it.

"Asshole!" she screamed.

I stood ramrod straight, I had broken bones before that had not inflicted this much pain.

"What do you want?" I said as softly as I could.

"I left my purse in your apartment you freak!" she shrieked.

I turned to face her, "You yell like that again and I'll peel your face off."

She was going to start ranting again, I had the feeling this was one of those women that thrived on drama but something in the set of my eyes must have let her know that this would become a CSI episode rather than anything on Jersey Shore.

"I just need to get my purse," she said in a tone that would ensure her survival.

I put my key in the lock, I swear I could hear every tumbler as they moved into place to unlock my door, I winced as each and every notch became engaged.

"Hurry up," bitch said. "I don't want to be seen out here with you."

I turned the knob, the latch scraping against the door frame reverberated up through my arm and into my head. What's her name pushed past me to get in.

"Come on in," I growled to her swaying ass. I could still appreciate her form, I wasn't dead, just a skull splitting headache.

"Got it!" she yelled from my bedroom, I almost fell to my knees. I was still standing in my entry way as she came out of the room. "I thought clowns were supposed to be jolly and shit," she said as she looked through her purse. "I could take care of that, if you want."

I knew what she was implying. "You just called me a freak," I whispered.

"That was for anybody watching, you've got one of the biggest cocks I've ever seen and I'm already here."

I shrugged. "Fine." Refer back to the part where I said I wasn't dead. I started to unbuckle my suspenders.

"Leave them on," she said sultrily. "I've always wanted to do a clown."

Chicks are by nature flawed beasts—who am I to deny them? She retreated back into my bedroom and I followed. I unzipped my fly to give her better access.

"Come here, lover," she said from my bed.

Shit how long did it take me? She was already naked and waiting, either I had lost some time or she was just that practiced at the maneuver. I decided not to dwell on it. Of course she was a slut; if I had picked her up for a one night stand probably a dozen or so other guys had too. As blood flowed from my big head into my little one, the pain subsided somewhat in my brain, I made sure to shove as much of me into her mouth as possible to keep her from talking. The less she said, the better I felt.

Eventually, I got on top of her supporting my weight on my forearms, her head rocked back and forth as I thrust into her, with her mouth slightly open she began to moan, at first softly, and that was a magnificent turn on. I thrust harder and faster, her body and head began to shake violently from her orgasmic convulsions, her encouragement for me to come, became shrill infestations in my ears. The pain that was being held at bay now rushed full force like stampeding bulls across the tender flesh of my temples. My forearms gave way, but still I humped her for all I was worth. The pleasure of the sexual act was the only thing that was keeping me functional from the crippling pain.

I knew somewhere far in the distance that placing all of my bulk on her was a burden, but she would have to suffer through it until I was done.

She was here for my enjoyment. At first I could feel her sag under the added pressure and then she began to fight against me. She had punctured through my outfit and flesh in more than one spot with her fingernails in a desperate bid to get out from under me. At some point she was able to move her head far enough that she was able to bite on my cheek and ear, still the pain of her defensive posturing did little to break through the cloud of misery that scraped along my mind.

It was her shrieking that finally did it. It was like someone took the head of a needle and was slowly dragging it across my eyeball, I pulled out of her completely and raised up as she took a huge ragged breath of air. When I came out of my pain filled abyss, I crashed back down and into her, I angled my head so that my mouth was by her neck.

'Eat!' tore through my head, the message lit up across my mind like my own personal bat signal. I wasn't even hungry, between the pain in my head and screwing a hot chick I didn't see much chance of fitting a peanut butter and jelly sandwich in.

'Hungry!' The insistent thought cramped my belly, and was making my penis go from wood rigid to pasta soft.

I still had cognitive thought as I tore a chunk of her throat out roughly the size of a hamburger slider, but my motor skills were rapidly slipping from my control. Her eyes were glazed with pain and shock as blood pumped through the wound. I kept thrusting my deflating penis and biting, thrusting and biting, blood soaked my face, and it pooled around her head and still I kept pumping. I came with a shudder just as her eyes fluttered closed. My vision tunneled and I crashed down on what was left of her one last time.

***

It was nighttime when I finally awoke. "What the hell is going on?" I asked myself. I tried to wipe the sleep from my eyes. The pain, the blessed pain was gone. I wanted to do a dance I felt so good. I vaguely remembered the events of the day, that stupid little kid biting me and then coming home to what's her name.

'Oh shit, is she still here? I'm not taking her out, maybe she just left.'

I could hear what sounded like a dog chewing a particularly succulent bone, but since I didn't own a dog I would have to move on to the next explanation.

"Am I dreaming?"

I couldn't move, my eyes were open and I was looking through them but I was so close to whatever was in front of them that I could not focus properly. 'Did that bitch drug me? She's probably robbing me while I lie here like a log.'

"I'll kill you bitch," I screamed, but I don't think my mouth was working.

'Whoa that was fucking weird!' My body moved and I didn't do it. I screamed next, for how long I don't know but my throat should have been shredded by the time I was done. The brief glimpse I caught of what's her name, before I closed my eyes was horrifying. Her face was gone, picked clean as if she had been lying in the desert exposed to all the wild animals for a week. One eye was gone and the other was bit cleanly in two. The skin around her neck had been peeled like an orange except for a few deep wounds where chunks of meat had been torn loose.

I was puking, but I wasn't. I could FEEL myself retching but my body was not responding. Then my traitorous body descended back down onto the prone form of the woman and pulled another meager strip of skin from her forehead. The wet smacking sounds as I chewed the flesh was nauseating, I could hear *myself* swallowing but no matter how hard I tried to force it from going down my gullet still it happened. My body was ravenously hungry, even as I was convulsing in disgust.

"Am I dead? This must be hell. The bitch killed me!" I yelled. "But why would I be eating her then, that doesn't make any sense," I was a disembodied voice stuck in my body. I had no form, I was nowhere and I was nothing yet here I was. My body continued to rend through the carcass of Gina, yeah that was her name, Gina Talgera. Great, NOW is when I decide to put a name to the strips of beef I'm eating. This just can't be real, now I told you I was an offensive lineman in football, not a famed position for having to think but I was going to, NO, I needed to reason this out.

So either I'm dead and this is some form of hell, possible. I'm asleep and I'm having one hell of a believable dream, again possible. Or I'm alive and my consciousness is now trapped in a cannibalistic body, out of the three scenarios this one is the least believable. So the best I can hope for is that this dream does not drive me insane and that I wake up in a few hours and kick this crazy bitch out of my house because apparently she slipped me some sort of mickey that is having some sort of serious mind-fuck on me. Maybe I'll slap her around a little before I let her leave just because of what she's putting me through.

I peered out of my eyes, which were not mine to control just as my body ripped a breast free with an audible sucking sound. "Fuck! This feels real," I yelled as jets of saliva shot in the back of my throat. My teeth gnashed through the fatty material, my hand grabbed onto the voluminous piece of flesh so that I could tear pieces from the handful of beef. I reached out with my mind for that was the only tool I had available. I could 'sense' my body, could see and hear through my eyes and ears. I could feel my hands, sticky with blood; could feel Gina's intestines as my hands grabbed large portions, could feel my muscles strain as they pulled parts of her free. I could feel my teeth as they tore into slick casing, I blacked out momentarily as I allowed myself to 'feel' the taste as the coppery, shit taste flooded through my mouth.

Occasionally, my head would whip up from time to time in accordance to the cacophony of sounds that were exploding outside and I could catch brief glimpses of my alarm clock before it completely went out. But it was much easier to keep watch on the sun that blazed through my window. It was Saturday when the bitch had come to get her purse, two sunrises later and my unresponsive body had completely picked her clean. Somewhere deep inside myself I was slightly impressed, I had consumed fifty to fifty five pounds of meat a day. There was nothing left of Gina except for her skeletal remains—oops scratch that—and two bags of silicon. Yup, definitely going insane, because I laughed like a loon for the next ten minutes. Apparently, there is nothing funnier in the world than the sight of the remains of a devoured body with two silicon bags left over because yes, even cannibals have their standards.

My body stood, fully upright for the first time since I had started to bang the bitch, I was heavy with the weight of her. And then my body let loose easily one of the most voluminous blasts of gas ever. Even in this state I had wished that I had caught it on tape or at least had a witness, Gina didn't count, she was dead and I was pregnant with her remains. For a count of 47 Mississippi I ripped ass, I've got to admit even under the circumstances it was magnificent. I took a chance and allowed myself to tap into my sense of smell. I immediately regretted the decision, it smelled exactly like what you would expect a decomposing body to smell like. Rotten fucking meat enshrouded in shit. I couldn't close that doorway quick enough. And then it got worse, the farts turned liquidy, I was shitting down my leg, pools of the thick liquid were gathering at the bottom of my pants where my elastic cuffs were holding it back. I could feel the tepid substance as it began to seep and leak through the choke point, within a minute I could feel my feet completely covered.

It got worse, the liquid escaping my bowels tapered off to be replaced by more solid waste material, logs of offal began to course down my thighs and calves. Unlike the liquid the chunkier material could not escape the trappings of my clothes and began to bunch up around my lower legs. I cajoled and begged and screamed at my hands to take my pants off so that I could get in the shower. Nothing happened, my body was immobile as I was apparently disposing of Gina in her entirety. I guess I could call her a piece of shit and mean it now.

I don't know how much longer I stood there, I had stopped counting when my body had switched from gas to solids, but at least ten minutes later the release stopped, I blessedly moved from the location. My head scanned the room, the splatter of blood, gore, bile and shit looked like someone had dropped a grenade in a B-movie prop department. There was too much of everything—it couldn't be real, even the portion of hair attached to scalp that was stuck to the wall, it was all just overkill. One body could not make this much evidence, and then I seized up–that's what this was now, one major fucking crime scene. I would never be able to hide this much. FIRE, welled up in my mind, my only chance was to burn everything. Great thought, but I couldn't even make my hands scratch my nuts if the desire so came. Which now that it was on my mind was the single act that I most wanted them to do. My left nut was stuck to my thigh, I was trying to not think of WHAT it was stuck with just that it needed to be let free and it itched uncontrollably, my body paid it no mind at all. Which in a sense made sense, because I was the mind and my body was not paying me any heed.

I flipped the sensory switch off, better to not feel at all than to feel that. Relief was sweet but the back of my mind still tickled with the phantom itch. This was the first time I could ever remember in my life of hating my own balls. Sure there were the times I had taken a shot to the nuts and dropped to my knees, but even with my legs drawn in and my stomach threatening to heave, I didn't hate them, I cherished them even more, fearful that now they might somehow have suffered a damage that would not allow them to work properly. But right now they were shit-encrusted globules that pushed me that much closer to the edge. For insanity was the line I was straddling of that I was sure.

My body began to pace around my apartment, apparently in search of more sustenance. It banged up against the fridge a few times but then seemed to lose interest. Around and around we went, where he stops nobody knows, (and then I laughed maniacally in my head). Yup, no matter which way this panned out I was going to end up in a room padded with loads and loads of rubber or foam. The constriction of the straight jacket couldn't be any worse than what I was going through now, at least my arms would be mine to not move.

I tuned back into the senses of the creature that looked like me but wasn't, we, he, it was staring out the window at a particularly succulent looking fat man running for his life with a dozen or so something's chasing him. Now why would I call a fat man succulent?

My senses were ripped to the fore as an all consuming gnawing clawed through my belly. I was so hungry it was all I could think about. The hunger was a tangible entity it was threatening to rip its way through my bowels until it found solace. 'Must feed'. It said over and over. I severed that connection at this point I figured it was just better to stay with the eyes and the ears. And even that was two senses too many.

My head ripped around as a soft tapping came to the front door. "Tim, are you there?" came an even softer voice.

"Dad? Dad? Get the fuck out of here!" I screamed, sure it was only in my head but it was still loud. I was petrified of what my old man was going to think if he saw me like this, he didn't know I made extra money as a clown! My body moved closer to the delicious smells pouring forth from under the door. 'I shut smell down!' I thought. Every tumbler as it clicked into place was like sweet ambrosia to my hulking alter ego self.

"Oh, dear God. What is that smell?" my father asked as he opened the door and quickly slid in, making sure to reengage the lock before turning around to survey my place, which was bathed in the shadows of twilight. A partially cloud-shielded full moon could not hide the nightmares that awaited Liam (my father) as he looked down my hallway.

"Timothy? Tim, you're alright." My father said with relief. "Tim?" He asked as I kept approaching him soundlessly. I passed by the mirror I had in the hallway, I looked through my peripheral vision, because my zombie self's eyes never strayed from their target. I was the stuff of nightmares. A giant zombie clown bathed in blood and shit—fuck other people, I wasn't going to be able to sleep for a week after seeing that.

"Tim, you look horrible," my father exclaimed as he backed up into the door he had just moments before closed. I watched as his hand slid up, trying to find the locking mechanism. The old man was quick but not quick enough, my body sensed that its next meal was about to flee . My dad placed his hands up, which I summarily began to chew through, I could hear my front teeth shatter as they crashed down upon his wedding ring. I don't know why he still wore the damn thing, I got my philandering ways from my father, the difference was I didn't pretend to be married.

I couldn't believe how incredibly good his fingers tasted once I swallowed the wedding ring, the pinkie ring and the watch, almost choked on that garish thing. My father's screams didn't stop until I was halfway up his wrist by which time it became more of a high keening. Then ceased all together. My body quivered with the delight as it rendered mercilessly through his body, I had long retreated to a dark recess. Maybe not as soon as I should have but I went, eventually. There was a measured sense of satisfaction as I killed my father—he was an asshole, plain and simple. His idea of love usually revolved around a beer buzz and the back of his hand—that was of course until I turned fourteen when I became bigger than him.

The only reason I can figure he even came over here was for me to protect his scrawny little ass, it wasn't to make sure I was alright. My father blamed me for all the ills in his life. Most fathers past their prime try to live vicariously through their kids, not my old man, though. He wanted his old life back and he saw me as the roadblock that prevented him from getting back there. When I was eight years old he had locked me in the basement for a solid week. I was old enough to realize that crying out would have brought more wrath than mercy. Not once did he check on me to see if I needed anything or if I was even alive. The day after Christmas I heard the bolt slide back on the basement door and then he had just left, most likely to the bar with his friends. Luckily, my mom had been sort of a canning freak in those last few years she had managed to stay with the old man and to this day though I cannot eat, pickles, beets or sweet relish. I get the cold sweats when I pass jars of them at the grocery store. My hands and piss smelled like vinegar for the rest of the week, every time I rubbed my eyes they would burn for hours.

Before he went out he had left me a can of Pabst Blue Ribbon on the table and on a napkin he had scrawled 'Merry Christmas Shithead, save the can for redemption'. I thought about crying as I looked through the kitchen window and out into the daylight, but as I drank that beer down I swore I would someday pay him back for that.

***

It was many hours later before I dared borrow my senses just because this was the second person I had eaten. Didn't mean that I had gotten used to it.

'I'm blind!' I screamed, and that was terrifying. I was already a prisoner in my own body but now I couldn't even see! As I controlled my faux breathing, trying to suppress the panic that was welling up in me I began to sense a soft light. The harder I concentrated the brighter it got before I realized that dawn was approaching. My body was pinned up against the front door; that was why I couldn't see anything except the dark maple stained pine.

My dipshit body couldn't figure out how to get out of the apartment and apparently, I was starving again. Three hundred or so pounds of meat in two days just wasn't good enough, it's not like they were Chinese.

'Turn the knob, fuck head!' I yelled.

My head whipped quickly from side to side and then up and down like it was looking for what had spoken to it.

'Holy shit! Fuck wad, can you hear me?' That head movement came back. This could get interesting. It beat the hell out of quivering in the dark like a victim.

'Hey big fella, can you turn the knob?' The head movement happened again but it wasn't nearly as pronounced. Whatever was controlling my motor functions had at least enough of a thought process to potentially realize that whatever was talking to it was internal. I sensed 'feelers' wriggling through the ripples of my mind.

It... they were looking for me and they would devour me much like they had my dear old dad. I pictured my hidey hole as a room, a small black dark room which I immediately closed the heavy iron door to, just as the 'feelers' slid on by. I was tempted to *make* a moat but I didn't want any undo activity to cause anything to come investigating.

'Fuck you!' I yelled. The feelers halted their progress, their heads all shot up like prairie dogs in their dens. I covered my mouth lest it betray me. Being like this sucked, it sucked bad but being dead was worse. I was pretty certain that there was no afterlife, no God to atone to and I had lived my life accordingly, but always something niggled 'what if I'm wrong?' in the back of my mind. Best to just delay any mythical meeting with this person; now that two murders were on my resume. Although, if my feet were really held to the fire I'm not sure how I could be held accountable for them.

The worms/feelers were still moving around but much slower as if they had caught a scent. I held my breath, figuratively and turned, listening to the noise as a worm scraped up against my door, it had found my hideout. The noise traveled farther up the closure. It was raising its head to let its brethren know. The first thing I could think of was 'sword'. I nearly dropped the two handed broadsword that appeared. I imagine it would have been in the neighborhood of fifty pounds. The steel shone bright and was encrusted with gems of varying colors and sizes, it looked a lot like the one Arnold used in the *Conan* movie.

The worm turned to look at me as I opened the door and rushed at him. Although, 'look' is a stretch—it didn't have anything resembling eyes. The thing that stared at me was roughly humanoid, it looked like something a retarded five year old would draw. 'Fuck you!' I screamed again as I swung my sword clipping the end of its stinger. Caustic fluid flowed from the wound and I watched in horror as wherever the blood came into contact with my mind, the pinkish matter turned gray. This thing was destroying in moments what I had planned to do over the span of many years with booze, pills and definitely some grass.

I brought my sword back up, the man-shaped thing in front of me was struggling. I had not incapacitated it. Whatever this was, it was safe to assume it was a battle to the death, I brought my sword crashing through its fuzzy head quickly stepping back lest I get any of that poison blood on me. But the white fluid that ran from its head was not made of the same material, it merely coursed through the channels in my mind. The thing collapsed to the ground, that's when it hit me. 'Dumb ass, why didn't you just wish for a *gun*?' Dozens of various weapons began to form in my hands, I settled on the AA-twelve, yup, a fully automatic twelve gauge shotgun, that would work perfectly.

'Fuck this cowering shit—I'm going on the offensive.'

I could sense movement all around me they were coming. 'Be careful for *their* swords,' I heeded that advice unlike my mom's advice to be nice to women and they would be nice to me. Chicks are flawed animals, the worse I treated them the more they came around. I had once sodomized a girl who had begged me to stop, had to throw my sheets away she had bled so much on them. She had called me for a month straight trying to go out on a second date, I had finally picked up the phone and told her I'd had better. I'm fairly certain I had heard from one of my friends that she had moved to Seattle or maybe killed herself, I don't know never really cared enough to get any further explanation.

I let lead fly, the 'men' fell all around me, only one got close enough to make it interesting, his head disintegrated for the effort. I felt like Rambo, hell I think I was screaming like him. I was blowing thousands of imaginary rounds through an imaginary weapon, never worrying if my barrel would overheat or if I would run out of bullets, it was damn near orgasmic.

What came next finally made me stop holding the trigger down. I could feel my invaders looking through my mind for something. It was unnerving, all attention had been diverted away from me, the sound that emanated from my mouth could hardly be considered speech, it sounded more like a rake being dragged over bones.

"Truce?" Came the sound from my mouth, using my thoughts to talk to me.

Was this a trick? 'What, so I'm kicking your ass—you want me to give up? Fuck you!' I shouted to myself.

I was allowed to sense 'men' by the millions amassing for an assault. I began to wonder if I could call in an air strike.

"Truce?" Came the one word question again.

'Stop talking!' I told myself. 'Girls in the morning sound less irritating than you!' I stood for a moment as I lost concentration the gun I had fabricated quickly dissolved into the material it was made out of. 'I want my body back!' I yelled.

"Must feed." Was my only response to myself.

'You fat bastard, you just ate two whole people—how much more do you need?'

"Must feed." My tortured voice box repeated.

And then it hit me, whatever had control of my body needed my help, the dipshit couldn't figure out how to open the door. "So you're pretty much asking me if I'll drive," I said.

"Feed," it pleaded with me.

I took too long in my thoughts. "Feeeeeeeeeeeeeeeeeeeeeeeed!!" it keened.

'Shut up!' I said placing my hands over my ears, about as effectual as pissing on a forest fire.

"Feed, feed, feed, feed!"

I think it would have gone on forever or until me or it died. I wasn't willing to find out just how long that might be.

"Turn the knob!" I told it while also imagining how the process looked.

My alter ego composed self, wrenched its gaze down to its hand and grasped the handle, it turned the lock so hard I could hear the innards snap, I had a moment of panic thinking that I would be stuck for eternity in this dark shell while Bozo here cried for food.

'Pull!' I shouted before it completely tore up the inside of the door.

A drunk eighty-year old with Alzheimer's would have reacted faster to my command but at least it did as it was told. I personally would have stopped to take in the carnage that was all around me but my other self had other ideas. Smoke from fire, ruined cars smoldered, people or things lay in various states of decay. Bullet casings littered the ground, more than once we almost lost our footing on them.

'We?' When had that thought crept into my head? It was still my enemy and I would do whatever it took to get my self back.

'What are you?' I asked the thing in control of my body. But if it couldn't turn a door knob, could it be self aware? I doubted it. It might not be smart by my definition but he/it was most assuredly running the show, he had taken complete control of me. I was thinking about what it could potentially be; an alien, a demon, a germ, or maybe a virus. I had once read on the internet about a zombie virus that the government had been working on during World War II,-called operation Hugh Mann, but I had skimmed over most of it and considered it to be just more conspiracy bullshit. I wouldn't have read it at all if it weren't for the fact that I had to click away from porn as my boss came out of his office to check on all his good little worker bees in Cubicle City. Even as I had struck an answer I shied away from it, I had just eaten two people and I had no control over my own extremities but the fact that I was a zombie still hadn't hit home.

"Holy shit, Vern, do you see that one?" I heard a man shout from across the street.

"That is one big fuckin' zombie," came another voice that I could only imagine belonged to Vern.

My head turned to look at two older men who both looked like they had just ransacked an Army surplus store. How they figured their camo outfits were going to make them blend in with the coffee shop front was beyond me.

Hugh, yeah that's what I'd call my body. Seems fitting somehow. Hugh picked up their scent and was off to the races. The look of surprise on Vern and the other guys face was pretty hilarious right up until the other guy lifted his huge rifle into place.

'Hugh, whoa!' I screamed. 'Fucking stop, you ape! You're going to get us killed!'

"That sum' bitch is fast, Darryl. You'd better hurry up and shoot it."

"Sum' bitch?"

"You know what I meant. Shoot that thing."

"Did you mean son of a bitch?"

"Whatever! Shoot the fucker!" Vern screamed.

I was halfway across the street, Darryl had a bead right on my forehead, I swear I could feel the laser dot painting me like an Indian bride. I told Hugh to sidestep just as the first shot rang out. I was pulled to the side as the bullet crashed into my shoulder. I hesitantly waited for the onrush of massive amounts of pain. What came would barely be considered as painful as a mosquito bite.

"The head, Darryl! The head!"

"I did shoot him in the head—he moved. He's so *fast*."

Darryl dropped his weapon down, pulling the bolt up. The hot brass tinkled to the ground. He was struggling to put a fresh bullet into the action. Who the fuck brings a bolt action rifle to a zombie fuck fest?

Darryl had a look of triumph on his face as he brought his rifle back to bear, unfortunately for him it would be a short lived. Hugh was already past the barrel of the rifle and used Darryl's body to stop our forward momentum as we crashed into the store front window. Shards of glass, some as big as flagstones, rained down all around us, Darryl seemed to have gotten the worst of it. Between the pieces of glass sticking out at odd angles and his fleshy lips being chewed up in my mouth he wouldn't live long.

"Darryl! Fuck, Darryl! You alright?" Vern shouted behind me.

'Yeah, dipwad, he's fine,' I thought as Hugh ripped through his left eye. 'And he's getting better all the time.' There was no reason on Earth that I should be getting used to eating people, but hey, I was just along for the ride.

'Darryl would be alive now if you hadn't shown Hugh the way out.'

'Who the fuck said that?' Great, another mouth to feed, so to speak. For solitary confinement, it was beginning to get real crowded. There was still the chance that all of this was insanity; maybe one of the many skanks I had used had returned the favor and given me a virulent dose of syphilis. And if you didn't already know, I'll tell you—untreated syphilis rots your brain. So let that be a lesson to you kiddies brought to you by Spangles the clown. I was cracking myself up right until Hugh chewed through the man's lower intestine. I could have gone the rest of my life, such as it is, without ever having to have seen Darryl's half digested hot dog. 'Ever hear of chewing!' I screamed at the corpse that I had my head buried in. What was worse was when Hugh ate it. Images of my head buried in a toilet bowl flooded my mind. Hugh picked up on the plethora of images and he also began to vomit.

Eating a raw human was absolutely disgusting, puking one back up was beyond description. I slammed the door to my 'room' and all my senses just as Hugh began to dive back into his work, throw up and all. If I knew where my knees were I would have been in the corner holding on to them rocking back and forth. Could this really be happening? Vern had called me a zombie, sure I had watched Dawn of the Dead as a kid but I don't remember there being any exposed breasts in the movie I had quickly lost interest in the genre. I started to rattle through my extremely limited information relating to this new development. I was fairly certain they ate brains, but Hugh had already proved that wrong, he ate everything even that fucking half a hot dog. I almost hurled again.

Zombies were slower than that lineman *after* I had destroyed his knee. No, that's not right either because we had been flat out running across that street after Vern and Darryl. So everything I knew about zombies was false or Vern was wrong. I couldn't really ask him for clarification now, could I? I started to laugh and so did Hugh. Only when a giant clown covered in blood and gore does it, it's not nearly as funny. After what seemed an appropriate time I lifted the shades to my senses, Hugh was almost at a blissful balance between sated and hungry. But he was worse than a Hummer traveling down the highway at eighty miles an hour, I could watch as his hunger gauge began to tip.

Hugh looked around, Vern had departed to places unknown once he realized his friend was not quite alright.

'Hungry,' formed in my thoughts, followed by the feeling of vast emptiness.

'They'd never let you in to an all you can eat buffet,' I told him.

'Food,' Hugh thought.

'Go fucking get it,' I told him. 'There's nothing in your way.'

'Hungry.'

He wanted me to take a more active role in our hunt. I could damn near rationalize showing him how to open the door and sidestepping the bullet but this was a whole different thing altogether. This was active participation in savagery, in cannibalism, in murder. According to the two things on my checklist I was not a zombie no matter what Vern and Merle thought, what harm could come from my helping Hugh out? Maybe it would make me wake from this nightmare quicker or submerge me deeper so I wouldn't have a self left either way was better than this limbo.

'Get up, asshole.'

He did as I said. I stretched out my senses a bit more. Damn, I was heavy. Vern was easily two hundred fifty pounds and I had consumed at least a hundred fifty pounds of him, hotdog and all. I might be strong but hefting another man inside my belly was only going to slow me down.

'Waste elimination,' I told Hugh.

He formed a crude '?' in reply.

'Fine, have it your way,' I told him, I projected my thoughts to show him how to take a proper shit, magazine and all. He didn't get the irony as I made sure to be holding a Fine Dining periodical I thought it was hilarious. Bricks of shit began to fill up in my pants, bulging the already stretched fabric to its limit. I was going to interrupt Hugh in this most private of endeavors, I really was, but I thought better of it, not because I gave a fuck about him, but I still had my standards, and running across the city with shit-filled pants was way better than being naked from the waist down. Dignity I would hold on to for a little while longer.

Runny blood-brown liquid began to seep through my pants, the gold coloring of the pants had long since vanished, replaced completely with a color close to that of three day old road kill. Didn't much matter the animal they all turned the same color eventually.

A twenty second long burst of aroma that would kill a skunk tore through my anus, signifying an end to the evacuation of Vern from my bowels.

'Hungry,' Hugh repeated.

'You're going to have to work on your vocabulary,' I told him as I turned him to face a direction I knew would be stockpiled with food. The weak-minded always thought their God would protect them during the end of times; Hugh and I were about to show them otherwise.

'Eat now.'

'Much better, Hugh! Don't worry, my friend, church will be packed this time of day,' I said, laughing maniacally. Hugh was too determined to enjoy in the revelry. 'You missed a good one,' I told him, wiping an imaginary tear from my eye.

I wasn't the only one with this idea the church was surrounded by some of the foulest creatures this planet could produce. I won't lie, I got pretty scared first that they might try to eat us and when that didn't happen that they might notice Hugh wasn't exactly the same as them and still try to kill him. We passed some zombies (I'll use that for lack of a better term) who were in some serious state of disrepair. One looked like he had been sawed in half and still he dragged his exposed spinal column across the pavement. A woman zombie was bent at the waist, looking like she had been hit by a car and it had fractured her back or hip—*something*—but still she shuffled to the feast. Some had bite wounds, others blunt trauma wounds, knife stabs, sword slashes, and most of the injured had bullet wounds.

How could any of them survive this much damage? It was then that I remembered the shot we had got from Vern. I forced Hugh to look down at the wound it wasn't bleeding. Hugh wrenched control back so that he could approach the front doors. I made him move his left arm, there was no pain. No grinding of bone on bone, no sprung leakers, it was as if it had never happened.

'How?' I asked Hugh.

Hugh stopped walking for a moment as he tore through my memories. 'Fix. Eat now.'

'Fucking-A, you're an insurance company's walking wet dream.'

We were halfway through the throng of flesh-worshippers, when I realized that not a one of these monsters gave a rat's ass about us. But the multitude of rifles pointing through the now smashed stained glass windows surely did, and as tall and brightly dressed up as I was, I was quickly going to become a target.

'Turn!' I shouted to Hugh.

'Hungry!' he screamed like a spoiled child.

'Dead soon if you keep going.' I flashed images of our body lying in a pool of blood with a caved in skull.

'No dead,' Hugh said. 'Hungry.'

'I'll get you your damn food but we're going to do this my way!' I said.

Hugh reluctantly agreed and turned away and not a moment too soon. The zombie that thought he had just won the lottery by getting our spot fell to the ground with a bullet hole in its forehead. Hugh never turned around as the dead zombie's body slammed into ours. 'Faster,' I urged. Hugh obliged, but only because he knew this meant food sooner. Someone sure had a hard-on for us. Zombies all around us began to take on wounds even as we pulled away from the major push of them. I knew we'd attract attention but shit we were easily a hundred yards from the church and still I had to make my hulking frame weave and dodge to avoid the stinging missiles as they zipped by. As it was, Hugh's minions were going to be busy fixing the two or three that had caught up to us. Hey, I was an offensive lineman, not a running back. Either the guy was out of bullets or we had finally pulled out of his effective range. I waited until we were out of sight of the church before I made Hugh turn around, this time we were going to come up from behind.

Hugh might be hungry but I was plain old pissed off. What the fuck had I done to make that guy try and kill me, unless he was the boyfriend of some girl I had boinked, who was I to him? I sure as hell didn't ask to be a flesh-eater. Or maybe he just hated clowns; I actually found that more acceptable reason to loathe me. I was going to pull out and eat his liver while he watched! Holy crap where did that thought come from?

'Hugh? Did you do that?'

'Hungry.'

'Quite the conversationalist, aren't you?'

Amateurs, I thought as I had Hugh open the door at the back of the church. I'm no military man or even one of those half-crazed survivalists, but hell, even I know enough to watch my six. The corridor was darkly lit and narrow, depictions of Jesus in varying forms of torture lined both walls. Good thing he died for the sins I was about to commit. It was so dark we nearly stumbled over the 'guard' they had put at the back entry. The guy looked more like a zombie than half the ones out front. He was so friggin' old, a super market wouldn't hire him to be a greeter at their store. You know the guys I'm talking about, one foot in the grave and the other dangling precariously over the edge. They're about as intimidating as a new born with a rattle, who do they think they're fooling, I don't give a shit if they were once a cop or a war hero, makes no difference, they're old and useless now.

I almost had to laugh as Grandpa Moses eyes got nearly double their size as he saw me coming down the hallway at him. Geezer might almost be worm food but he brought his gun up faster than I would have thought possible, fucker still had a little juice in him after all. The first and only shot he got off nailed me in my pecker. 'You're going to pay for that!' I screamed in my head. Hugh crashed into the guy at a full-on sprint. I felt multiple bones crack under our assault as we drove him into the heavy wooden oak door that led into the church proper. Hugh had hit him so hard I didn't think there would be anything left to eat when he pulled back. I figured we'd just pressed him in to the wood. To forever become embedded in the grain. Somewhere in the fragmented pieces of my memory I was crying out in pain, the piece of my anatomy that my entire former life revolved around had suffered a grievous injury and Hugh didn't care as he bit down hard on Geezer's face, ripping off a strip of raggedy cheek meat.

'Eat,' Hugh said damn near gleefully.

"Jonas you okay?" a voice asked.

I might be slow but I figured out quickly who Jonas was as Hugh ripped through his neck.

"Jonas, answer me," a scared woman's voice demanded.

That's women, always demanding.

"Ben, Jonas isn't answering."

"Old turd is probably sleeping," Ben replied.

"Didn't you hear the gunshot?" the woman asked.

"Shit, Anna, if you haven't noticed there's about a million gunshots going off."

"From behind us?" she shot out.

"Well, check it out," Ben yelled to her.

"I don't have a gun."

"Fine, I'll be down in a sec to check, but I swear if he's sleeping, I'm kicking him outside."

'Hugh!' I was trying to gain his attention. Ben was coming and if he saw what was going on here we were both dead. Hugh was having none of it, though. He was pulling muscles off Jonas' thighs like they were succulent crab leg meat.

'Hugh!' I yelled again.

'Eating!' he yelled back.

'Very good, asshole using the present tense and all, but we're about to have company. And if my dick is still serviceable and I can somehow get control back from you I would like to make it through the next five minutes.'

Hugh was ripping the meniscus off of Jonas' knee. At this age I was surprised the old fuck still had any left.

"Jonas, Ben is coming. If you're asleep, please get up or he'll kick us both out."

"Oh no, not you, honey," Ben said. "You're entirely too fuckable and we'll need good hipped women like you to repopulate the planet."

"Pig," Anna cried. I could hear her retreating down the aisle way.

"Last chance, old man!" Ben shouted.

Hugh snapped his head up as Ben turned the door handle.

"What the hell?" Ben asked as he looked my hunched over form square in the face. I'm sure it was a hell of a sight with all that blood and gore dripping off me. Ben had initially let his weapon fall by his side from the shock but was now rapidly recovering. I launched Hugh forward trapping Ben's arm in the crushing vise of my body weight against the heavy door. I was almost able to shut the door once we had broke through the bones in Ben's arms. The rifle clattered to the floor. Hugh began to chew through Ben's arm as we kept our pressure on the door. His cries should have been drowned out by the shooting upstairs, but that bitch Anna saw what was happening and was screaming her lungs out. I was going to give eating her pussy out a whole new meaning.

Ben's major screaming had subsided it was mostly whimpers at this point but I'm sure someone on the other end was going to think something was a little fishy with one of their own trapped in the door. While Hugh was busy munching away, I wrenched the door open, grabbed a handful of Ben's head and pulled him into the hallway with us, but not before I gave little miss Anna my best 'Here's Johnny' gaze. She froze—it was brilliant!

"Anna, what's the matter?" somebody from upstairs yelled.

Nothing. Maybe she died of fright.

"Anna!" The voice yelled.

"There's a... there's a clown," Anna said softly.

"Anna, look at me!" the voice commanded. "There's a lot worse than clowns out there."

'Not this clown,' I thought. Hugh was crunching through one of our two victim's eyeballs.

"Where is Ben?" the voice asked.

Anna was in shock. She whimpered much like Ben had only moments before.

"In the hallway?" the man guessed.

Anna must have been pointing, maybe she was little tougher than I had given her credit for. As long as her flesh was tender that was all that really mattered right now.

"I'm going to come down and check."

Anna was hot, that was how she was getting two guys to come down and do a job she should have done. That's why the military didn't want women in combat. Guys would be pushing other guys out of the way so that they could fall on a grenade to impress the girl. Dipshits, the key to getting a girl is to be the one to throw the grenade at her, she'd come running at that point.

'Danger coming, Hugh.' Damn thing paid me no attention. I started flashing him images of guns and bullets.

'Pain... hurt,' Hugh thought.

Wow, so something does bother it besides hunger pangs. Hugh stopped rending through the old man's genitalia to look up at the door.

'Good boy, Hugh. More food coming.'

'Food good, Hugh hungry.'

"Don't!" Anna yelled in alarm.

Our new guest was a lot closer than I had anticipated.

"Jonas? Ben?" the man asked from right outside the door. "I'm going to shoot through this door if I don't hear either of you. This is no time for practical jokes."

Who does that? Who pulls tricks during an apocalypse? The new guy must have had an itchy trigger finger because he didn't give a second warning before he blasted two dime sized holes through the heavy door. Must be carrying a small cannon to get through that wood. The ass punched a hole through my ruffled collar. Not sure why I cared, it's not like I was going to be able to get the gallons of blood and shit out of the rest of the outfit anyway.

Thinking about shit triggered something in Hugh, he stood stock still as he began to evacuate his...I mean my bowels.

'Not now! Danger!'

'Need room to eat!' he yelled back at me.

I heard retching from the other side. "What the fuck is that smell?"

I didn't think it was that bad, maybe I was getting used to it.

"Frank! I think we got zombies in the hallway. Jonas and Ben are most likely K.I.A.

Anna was whimpering but she had moved farther away.

"Lock the door, Tom," Frank yelled down.

"No damn lock," Tom said. "Anna, come here. I need you to help me move this pew over."

I imagined her shaking her head because Tom asked her two more times for help.

"Tom, hurry up," Frank yelled. "We need you up here." "We're having a hard time keeping them from the front doors.

"Shit," Tom said. I heard him dragging something over to the door, didn't sound much bigger than a chair, probably the candle votive. The frame shuddered as he placed it up against the door and then I heard Tom beating feet to help his comrades in arms.

I smiled, I don't know if Hugh mirrored my gesture but if Tom had taken an extra second he would have realized the door opened inwards. Hugh kicked back into gear after dropping a good ten pounds of digested human.

'More food,' Hugh stated, looking at the door.

This was Hugh's way of asking me how to open the door. 'We need to wait. I can smell Anna from here, she's watching the door and if we come strolling through now, we'll die.'

I could sense Hugh was struggling with his insatiable need to feed and his desire to not get shot.

"Long how?"

'How long? Is that what you're asking, buddy? Do you have any concept of time?'

No response.

'Until it's completely dark, when the moon goes down.'

I think Hugh sighed but at least it wasn't the three year-old spoiled screaming that I was expecting.

'Want me to tell you a story to while away the time?' I asked him. He didn't respond so I took that as a sign to continue.

***

'I was eleven years old when Kevin Thompson went missing, I didn't do it but I didn't help, either. I was a big kid, bigger than most kids four and five years my senior, didn't have many friends back then.'

I stopped my narrative, now that I thought back on my life, I'd never had very many friends. Whatever.

'But that was why I was alone in the woods that day. I had just nailed a squirrel with a rock and its head was gushing blood. I was busy poking it with a stick; its legs were twitching like crazy. I looked up when I heard the muffled sounds of conversation not too far away. I wasn't scared when I went to check it out, just curious. Thinking back, I should have been afraid.

I knew these woods well. I'd been playing in them for the last four years, I knew how to get around certain obstacles and I knew how to be quiet. More than once I had been able to sit and watch as some teenagers from the high school partied or had sex. And a few times I had even watched as the high school quarterback boned a cheerleader or two. Even back then I didn't have a name for it or know exactly what they were doing, but I wanted to be doing it. Although I had on more than one occasion jerked off to the memory of that QB pounding the shit out of some girl. The memory was bringing about the painful realization that my manhood was most likely in tethers. I'm like every man on the planet, I love my penis. I'm not one of those crazies that name it or anything, but name me one other piece of the human anatomy that comes even close to the instant gratification that it delivers. Still waiting for an answer from Hugh on if he could mend it. I wondered how far Hugh's medical expertise extended.

'Hugh, fix my junk!' I demanded.

Nothing.

'Asshole!'

'Sleep!' he shouted back.

Wait, was he telling me to sleep or telling me that he *was* asleep? Ass wasn't even listening to my story. Might as well finish it, I wasn't going any place soon.

I was up on a small rise in a particularly dense copse of trees that gave a perfect view to the clearing below. There were four kids down there. I recognized a couple from the high school football team, although not the QB. There was Kevin and then some other guy who looked to be about the same age as the football players but he was way too stringy to play. The one I didn't know was dressed all in black, black boots, black shirt and weirdest of all was a black full length jacket, which in the middle of summer made no freakin' sense. I knew Kevin, he was in my grade. We ate lunch together a few times. He was nice enough and I almost thought to go down and say 'hi', but I don't know something just didn't feel right. First off, why he was even with these guys was strange, but that tall skinny kid had a look about him. I can't say back then I knew but I guess sinister is what comes to mind he had something planned out and it didn't bode well for Kevin.

"Where's the junked out car?" Kevin asked.

"We're close," Garrett, one of the football players said. He had a grin on that would have made the big bad wolf proud. It was entirely too toothy and his lips were pulled back way too far.

The other player, I think his name was Lyle looked like he wanted to be anywhere but here. Yeah, something wasn't right. I was with Lyle if I thought I could get out unseen I would have left too. I saw the glint of the shiny steel as the stringy kid pulled it out from a sheath on his belt. Kevin never saw it as Stringy stuffed it right into his gut, Kevin grunted like he had been punched. Stringy pulled the knife clear just as Kevin fell to his knees, he placed his hands over the wound in his belly.

"Oh fuck, oh fuck! What did you do?" Lyle yelled backing away from the scene. "You said we were just going to scare him."

"Well, he looks pretty scared, doesn't he?" Stringy replied.

"You know what I mean," Lyle said, his volume decreasing as Kevin's blood flowed.

Garrett's wolf grin seemed to be frozen on his face, I couldn't tell if he was enjoying the scene before him or not.

"Garrett, could you get my brother?" Kevin asked.

That must be how they got him here, Garret and Kevin's brother were friends. Man, in a world of messed up things, luring your friend's little brother into the woods to kill him has to rank pretty high up there.

"We... we can get him some help," Lyle said, approaching Kevin.

Stringy pulled his still glistening blade on the kid who was damn near twice his size. Lyle stopped short, I guess he knew that if the psycho would use it in cold blood on Kevin he wouldn't care a crap if he used it again on him.

Lyle tried a different tactic. "Garrett, come on man. This is Rog's brother, you've known him for almost his whole life."

"Yeah, I can't really stand the little turd," Garrett said, his face looking even more predatory.

"Polks, come on man, let's get him some help before this goes any further it's not too late."

At least I had a name for Stringy, not that I was ever going to tell anyone what I saw here, but still.

"It is now," Polks said, striking Kevin square in the throat with the knife.

Garrett laughed, and loudly drowning out Lyle's puking. Blood must have shot out a good five feet as Polks ripped the blade free. Kevin had a moment of indecision as he tried to figure out which flow he was going to try to stem. The crack as his nose snapped on a rock as he pitched forward was loud enough that the birds hightailed it from this area. Lyle stood up, brown bile coated the sides of his face.

Garrett turned Kevin over with his foot, frothy blood was running from the boy's mouth. "He's a goner," Garrett laughed.

"You say anything," Polks said, pointing at Lyle with his knife, "it will be your sister lying there and I'll make sure she doesn't die a virgin."

Lyle looked whiter than Kevin. Lyle could only nod his head, his sister was even younger than Kevin.

The three of them stood there a few moments longer before heading away. Lyle's head was bowed so much it was almost on his chest. Garrett looked like they had just won the state championship and Polks looked like he was ready for another victim.

I made sure they were long gone before I moved from my spot. I had been in the same position for so long my legs had gone numb, I straight-legged it halfway down the embankment before I lost my balance, I rolled to a stop face-to-face with Kevin, his pupils were the size of saucers and they were fixed on nothing as near as I could tell. I had just placed my hands under my chest and was beginning to rise when his pupils shrunk down to the size of pinpricks and this time they had found an object to latch on to...me. Sleeping legs be damned, I scurried so fast away from there I think I dug out a small rivulet.

"Please," he gurgled softly. His hand rose ever so slightly. There was not much of what made Kevin, Kevin, left. I wouldn't swear to it, but I thought I could see something, a white mist departing his body. All these years later I've tried to convince myself that it must be steam from the holes in his body but the mist originated square in the center of his forehead, not his throat. Never have been religious. I don't pretend to understand what others see in the divine but my existence within this body lends validity to what I saw that day. I would be that mist, of that I was sure.

I walked back over to Kevin slower than I had previously. To be honest, I was hoping he would just up and die before I got there. He was having trouble moving his head but those fucking eyes followed me all the way.

"I didn't do this," I told him nearly in a panic.

"Help... get," he eked out.

"Man, this is fucked up!" I told him. "I don't really want to get involved."

"Already are," he answered me. I could tell he was getting toward the end of his rope.

"You're the idiot that came into the woods with them. Polks is meaner than a woman with a cheap engagement ring (I'd heard that gem from my mother, I wasn't sure what it meant but it always made her laugh so I used it when it seemed right).

"Please..." Kevin managed.

Poor fucker, he was stupid enough to go into the woods with them, and then had the horrible luck to be discovered by someone who was too reluctant to help.

If I had helped him, he would most likely have made it. Sure, it would have been one hell of a scar on his neck but that would have been a small price to pay. He never uttered another word, but his eyes stayed on mine for the next three hours, never wavering. I was stuck now. I couldn't leave him. If by some miracle he got up and walked out of here or some other person stumbled upon him and rescued him he would rat me out. Wasn't I nearly as guilty at this point as Polks, Lyle, and Garrett?

The sun was close to setting and I had not checked in. I was going to have hell to pay for being late, plus I was famished. More than once, I looked around for a big enough rock to finish him off. I was trying to justify that I was going to put him out of his misery, but that wasn't true. I wanted him out of my misery. Those eyes would not stop watching me in that accusatory way.

I felt a small chill run up my spine the exact moment that Kevin seemed to have left his body, his eyes focused on nothing and he seemed forever frozen in a thousand yard stare. Maybe his departing soul had brushed up against me, I don't know, back then I was just happy that he wouldn't be able to get me in trouble. I ran home as fast as my legs would take me, I was terrified that I would end up for the night in those woods with Kevin and Polks. I didn't sleep much that night or the next few for that matter; I kept dreaming that Kevin was going to show up on my porch with his dead flat eyes and cold presence, demanding an answer. What was I going to tell him?

The cops found his body eight days later. Seems there wasn't much left to identify him, feral cats had got to his body. The little bastards had stripped him clean of all his meat from what I heard, now that's something I would have liked to have seen, from a distance. Within a few days of the discovery I was playing in my room when I heard the cops talking to my mom in the living room. I didn't even realize it at first but with my ear pressed to my door, my bladder had involuntarily loosed, hot piss ran down my leg and onto the rug.

"Yes ma'am, some of your neighbors said your son frequents the woods where Kevin Thompson's remains were discovered. We'd just like to ask him a few questions, maybe if he had seen something."

"My son hasn't gone to the woods in over a week."

'Oh shit' I was thinking, that sounds pretty suspicious to me and I'm not a cop.

"Is he a suspect?" My mom asked, almost like she was expecting them to reply,

'Yes he is public enemy number one.'

Now I know I'm not Johnny damn Appleseed but I'm not Al Capone, either.

"No ma'am, at this time there are no suspects, we are just trying to gather some information."

"Because that thing with the neighbor's dog was not his fault."

"Shut the fuck up, Mom," I moaned against the door.

"The dog, ma'am?" The cop asked.

"I mean, how does anyone call something that small a dog, anyway? Thing wasn't much bigger than a sewer rat and not much better looking, if you ask me."

"The dog, ma'am?" The cop asked again.

"Oh, that thing," my mom started up like she had completely forget about what she was talking about. "My Timmy was riding his bike when the rodent darted out in front of him. My poor Timmy almost fell off."

"What happened to the dog?" the other cop asked.

"Deader than a doornail, that thing was. My Timmy ran right over its head and my son is a big boy, crushed its skull right into the pavement. It was pretty grotesque, the thing's legs were all sticking up in the air, twitched for close to twenty minutes. The whole time the neighbor bitch is yelling at my Timmy and me. The cops actually hauled her away to calm her bitchy ass down. Now if she had a real dog like a Doberman pinscher or something you boys wouldn't be here trying to pin a crime on my son."

"Ma'am, no one is here blaming your son. Like my partner said earlier, we are just trying to see if your son saw anything suspicious while he was out playing."

"Like I said, he hasn't been out in those woods in over a week."

"Ma'am, Kevin Thompson went missing eight days ago."

I could almost hear the audible gasp my mother had produced at the coincidence in time frames. "Well, that means nothing."

'Nice recovery,' I thought sarcastically. My left leg felt cool as a breeze came in through my window, it was then I noticed the darker wet spot extending from my privates all the way down to my socks.

"Fuck," I mumbled. If the cops saw me like this they would just go and haul me off, only the guilty piss themselves.

I could hear my mom coming down the hallway as I frantically ripped my jeans off. I put on the first thing I could get my hands on, that it was Batman pajamas was inconsequential at this point. My mom entered without knocking, which was standard practice—and gave me the once over. Wadded up wet jeans in one hand and wearing pajamas at two in the afternoon, she had her suspicions but luckily she didn't say anything.

"There are some policemen here to see you," she said a little louder than she needed to. "Could you please get up and speak with them?" She turned so that she was facing back down the hallway. "He hasn't been feeling too good." Then she turned back to me, I think I saw a hint of fear in her eyes, like maybe she thought I could have had something to do with it. She'd never tell the cops that but things would forever be different between us—I was no longer to be her big teddy bear. From this point on she would always hold me at arm's length.

And the fucking dog had deserved it, thing nipped me twice. Now I didn't specifically go hunting the thing down like the neighbor lady said, but I also didn't swerve to avoid it when it came out to get me for the third time. I've got to admit it grossed me out when I crushed its skull but there was also a sense of satisfaction too, watching its brains leak out onto the ground, knowing that it was never going to bite me again. I wasn't expecting Mrs. Daniels to go quite so ballistic on me; she called me some names I'm still trying to figure out their meaning. By the time my mom figured out what was going on, the dog had just about stopped twitching and Mrs. Daniels was about to become even more volatile.

My mom pretty much sent me home before she jumped into the fray, looking back I don't think it had so much to do with Mrs. Daniels and the dog, it was more in the vein of 'if anyone is going to yell at my boy, it is going to be me'. Whatever, I didn't care all that much, I had put my bike up and gone back into the woods.

"Son, I know you don't feel so good," the first cop said to me.

I nodded, I bet I didn't look so good either, I was scared almost shitless, which was a good thing because if I crapped myself now that would just about be an admission of guilt. Confession by shit!

"Could you please tell me where you were on the twelfth? I guess that makes it last Monday," the thinner of the two cops asked.

"I... I think I was here," I answered honestly—who really knows what they were doing more than a week ago?

"What about earlier in the day, son, before it got dark? The day your friend went missing."

"He wasn't my friend," I said a little too hastily.

"But he was in your class, isn't that right?" The second cop who was by the doorway was beginning to look a little more interested in the proceedings.

"I guess but, there's lots of kids in my class," I said lamely.

"None that have gone missing, though." The first cop looked up from his pad.

I could feel more piss dribbling from my dick, luckily my bladder had been flushed mere moments before, unless they stared at my crotch I should have been alright. I started to shudder involuntarily.

"Look, he's sick with fever," my mother said, wrapping her arms around my shoulders. Looking back, I think it was more of a protection for her. If I confessed to something the stigma of her son being a murderer would be stuck on her; that was not something she could abide by. What would her bridge club think? "Unless my son needs a lawyer, I think that you two should leave until he feels better."

I watched as the two cops gave each other knowing glances, they knew something was up but neither one would ever return. The cop standing by the door, Officer Franco would die three days later as a petty thief named Wellington Conrad (strange name for a thief, should have been a Congressman) would decide that having a shoot-out with the cops for a whopping seventeen dollars he stole was infinitely better than spending any amount of time in jail. He got his wish, bleeding out on the street with three shots to the abdomen. He could have potentially been saved if the town's only ambulance wasn't busy transporting the dying Franco to the hospital, with a .22 long rifle caliber bullet lodged in his neck. His severed carotid artery pumped blood at a rate that would have dropped an elephant. Apparently, it had been a one in a million shot, Conrad had merely been shooting his gun up in the air trying to dissuade the cops from pursuit. After traveling a little bit over a mile straight up the bullet had been caught ever so slightly by a small breeze which pushed it off its trajectory and straight down into Officer Franco's neck. He left behind a wife, two young kids and a third on the way. That's what he got for making me piss my pants. A few months after everything blew over, I snuck out of my house with the sole purpose of going to the house of his widow and breaking out two windows. I hauled ass once I saw the lights turn on and at least one of the brats start to cry. Nowhere in this narrative did I say I was a good person, but the more I say the more I realize maybe just how shitty I truly am.

The second cop, Officer Dunleven, would become increasingly busy as the football player Lyle and his sister went missing at the same time. Polks must have thought he was too great a threat. Then a string of two more kids would never be coming home for Spaghetti Wednesdays. I don't know what happened to Polks at that point or why he stopped, I can't imagine that the evil within him was sated. Much like the Hugh(s) in me the evil would need to be fed constantly. Garrett, on the final play of his last game of his senior year, snapped his neck in two places. He'd be sucking smoothies through a straw for the remainder of his days. I never did have the courage later in life to check on Polks or his whereabouts; had suppressed it, in fact, these many long years. But most likely without the backing of Garrett and his muscles he wouldn't be able to lure much more than a wayward cat into those woods.

***

'Dark. Food.'

That startled the shit out of me.

'Can you open the door or do I need to show you again?' I asked Hugh.

'Do it! Hungry! So hungry!'

I had to tell myself to think these things out, if he was able to start learning I'd be out of a job and that meant he would redouble his efforts to get to me. As long as I was useful I was alive. Should have played the defensive line; they were the thinkers.

I had been so lost in my story I had not realized when the shooting had stopped but the church was eerily quiet. I would have preferred some noise something that would mask a door I was sure was going to be on loud squeaky hinges. Hugh relinquished almost all motor control on his right arm, it was nearly as easy to control it as it had been before I had been possessed. Maybe I should just choke the hell out of myself and escape from this fucking nightmare. Instead, I pushed the long handle down and pulled the door toward me, it slid open effortlessly and more importantly quietly. Anna's brown eyes seemed to gather ambient light and shine at me brightly from a few feet away where she was sitting at a pew, her attention rapt completely on the door I was now entering through.

"I knew you were still there," she sobbed quietly. "Nobody believed me."

I brought my index finger up to my lips, Hugh did not have the knowledge to make a 'shush' sound but the imagery still must have been terrifying. I smelled warm piss emanate from her direction, I was well aware of that odor. Hugh lurched over her way, Anna seemed caught between running like a rabbit and fainting like one of those Brazilian goats.

'NO!' I screamed to Hugh. 'She's last.'

'Eat her!' Hugh demanded.

'Soon my tapeworm friend.' I began to show him what I thought would happen if we started to munch on our little princess before we took care of the bang sticks. Hugh might have a few lights burnt out on his string of Holiday lights but he was bright enough to understand death.

'Can I use my vocal chords?' I asked. Hugh had no clue what I was talking about. This showing him everything that I needed to do to keep us alive shit was growing old. He released his grip on the entire neck region. Anna grew wide-eyed as my head plunged into my chest, I bet she was hoping I had died. I slowly seized control of the muscles and pulled it back up into a more respectable pose, her chagrin at my unexpected revival was pronounced.

My first attempt at sending air over my rigor induced vocal chords sounded like glass embedded in a cat's back being pulled slowly over a chalkboard. Anna pissed herself again, that was one healthy bladder and I was looking forward to tearing into it. I thought about going back into the hallway and clearing my throat to get this right, but Anna was under a spell at the moment and if I left now she would surely bolt. I kept pushing air until the bleeding cat glass sound turned to fingernails which in turn became the rough sound of a 40 year smoker who had swallowed small stones. It wasn't a pleasant or comforting sound but it got my point across.

"How many?" I asked pointing to the upstairs of the church.

Anna began to back up, she hadn't been expecting this new development.

"Anna," I croaked. "If you want to live, how many?"

Who the fuck believes a six foot five shit-and-gore covered talking clown zombie? A desperate, selfish woman, that's who.

"F-f-five," she stammered out quietly. "You'll let me go."

"I'll let you go."

'To meet your maker, if such a thing exists.'

She seemed pretty damned pleased that she had made a deal with me to save her own pathetic life, regardless of the fact that five others would have to pay the price for it.

'Eat!' Hugh demanded.

'No shit, you gluttonous fuck! I'm working on it.' That seemed to keep him quiet for the immediate moment. 'Now this is what is going to have to happen.' I laid out a plan for my carnivorous pal. He seemed to understand, as long as the pay-out involved meat he was good to go. Who knew zombies could adhere to the Adkins diet so well? Hugh would probably kill me if I made him eat broccoli.

"Anna, you all right down there?" a voice called out in the darkness. Shit, I was halfway up the stairs and with only one arm and my teeth as weapons I was vulnerable as hell. 'Anna, stay true to your normal self preserving self.' I screamed in my head.

There was an extremely long pause as for maybe the first time in her life Anna thought about someone else besides herself. Although that was maybe only half the truth, it was going to be who was going to better serve her needs. Oh I knew all about pretty women, the vast majority have never had to work for anything in their worthless lives. Look pretty and spread their legs and the world was theirs for the taking. I envied them for the ease with which they walked through life and loathed them at the same time. Oh yes, I was going to savor devouring her, if only she would stay true to form.

"Red..." she started. I was turning around—this wasn't looking good all of a sudden.

Red must have sensed something in her voice; I could hear him moving to come to her. Fuck, not much chance he was going to miss me in the middle of the staircase, not like I was going to blend in with the somber surroundings.

'Hugh, let go of the legs!' I yelled it so loud and maybe he could sense how close to disaster we were or at least how close I thought we were, but from the time of my request and his release it was seemingly a non-existent span. I ran up the remaining stairs. Red was just approaching the threshold, his rifle down by his side, it was long milliseconds that he took to recognize the threat fast approaching. He wasn't quick enough as I grabbed him around the neck with my right arm and pulled him close to rip his cheek off, careful to keep an increasing pressure on his neck so that he couldn't scream. He squirmed worse than a greased eel but I could bench close to six hundred pounds; he wasn't going anywhere soon. I lifted him higher and started tearing a shred of flesh from his chest, I had never in my life tasted a meat so juicy and succulent, the t-shirt he was wearing not hindering my eating experience in the least, must have been cotton.

Red's struggling peaked as I lifted him higher and tore into his sweet meats but began to come to a ceasing really quick as I tore his testicles off. A couple of days ago I would have told you that it was impossible for a human to tear through blue jeans with only their chompers but now I could say firsthand that is not the case. Although whatever Hugh was, human was not among the adjectives. Red became a ragdoll in my arms, as his life left so did his taste. Hugh and I were of the same mind that it was time to move on. I threw what remained of Red down to the bottom of the stairs, he landed considerably lighter than when he had originally alit them. Still, that bump in the night did not go unnoticed.

'Gotta be more careful,' I thought as I dragged the back of my hand across my face, spreading gore more than doing anything to get rid of it and that was actually alright with me.

"Did you hear that?"

"I didn't hear shit, shut the fuck up, I'm exhausted."

"Both of you shut up. Charlie you heard it; go see what it was."

"Who's coming with me?"

"Oh fucking pull your panties out of your snatch and go see," the first person that had spoken to Charlie replied.

"Maybe I didn't hear anything," Charlie muttered.

"Go fucking check it out or I'll shoot you myself, you sniveling little bitch." the third voice said.

He must be the leader. He needed to die quickly.

"Wait," a new voice chimed in. "Do you smell that?"

"Yeah it smells like zombies, if you haven't noticed, they're all around us," second man said.

"No shit, but this is stronger," fourth said.

"Like they're closer," Charlie piped up. I could tell from the sound of his voice that he was backing away from the stairs. The flight response was strong in this one. I heard at least two rifles come to the ready, maybe three.

"Help," I gurgled out, blood and viscera coating my vocal chords, my plea seemed to come out from under water.

"Who the fuck is that?" second asked.

"*What* the fuck is that?" third asked.

"Has he been bitten?" Charlie asked.

Three men peered down the stairs at me.

"Friend, I want you to come up slowly, hands stretched high."

I started to swallow quickly trying to force the meat and small bits of bone down. If I was going to pull this off I needed to sound somewhat normal.

'Hugh I need my other arm.' Hugh acquiesced; I didn't realize it then but I had control of nearly my entire body but all I could think about was that I needed to survive the next five minutes so that I could feast to my heart's content.

"Ooooweee, what the fuck are you, boy?" the leader said as I stepped up to the top of the stairs and into a small pool of lantern light. I held my hands up.

"Fucking shoot him," second said. "He ain't human."

"Please," I said. It wasn't perfect, but it wasn't horrible, either.

"Boy, you look like you came through the wrong end of a meat grinder," the leader said without mirth. His rifle never wavered from the top of my head.

"This is the only way I could get past them," I said pointing to all the blood on me.

The leader motioned to me to put my hands back up.

"Sorry," I told him.

"He don't look right," Charlie said from behind the leader.

"Even if he's human, which I'm not convinced." Third said. "He don't feel right."

"What's your story?" the leader asked me.

Hugh was literally shaking with the desire to move into action, I was struggling to keep him reigned in and still act good enough to keep us from getting shot. Something was going to have to give soon.

"Son, I asked you a question." The leader pulled the hammer back on his lever action rifle.

It just came to me, I don't know if I thought it or Hugh did, but it was going to buy me some precious seconds. "If you smell like them they won't try to eat you." That sounded plausible enough to me.

"Fuck, I think I'd rather die," second said, turning his head and holding his nose.

"Looks like you may have taken it a bit too far," the leader said. He wasn't buying it.

"The asshole is bigger than the jolly green giant," fourth said.

"Fred, I think you should just shoot him," second said to the leader.

"Shut up, Zak. I can't just shoot him yet."

"Merle, check his pockets for some ID," Fred said to fourth.

"Not fucking likely, Fred," Merle answered in no uncertain terms. "I read *IT* and this one is way scarier than the one I imagined in my head."

"I'll check him after you shoot him, maybe," Zak said and he wasn't kidding.

"Boy, you don't look good," Fred said.

"I'm covered in blood, shit and body parts from my neighbor. How do you think you'd feel?" I told him.

"Fair enough," Fred answered. "Why the clown outfit?"

"I wanted to blend in with the circus going on out there," I told him.

Fred actually laughed at that. "I still don't trust you much and if I weren't a God-fearing man locked in a church I think I'd rather send you on your way. But that is not the Christian thing to do.

"No way you're letting that animal stay here," Zak said.

"He can take your place," Fred said.

"Can I put my arms down?" I asked.

Fred nodded.

"Fred, what the hell are you doing? He's not human!" Merle said.

"Well he's not a zombie, either. Have you heard any of them down there asking for help?" Fred shot back. "Listen, friend."

"Timothy."

"Timothy, you smell to high Heaven, no pun intended. There is a bathroom and a small shower which you might be able to just squeeze in. I think your look and your smell are keeping the rest of our merry band from seeing the person beneath. If you clean up some I think we might be able to move further in our goal toward trust. Charlie, Merle, why don't you two escort him to where it is." He said it in a way that left no room for debate. Charlie looked chagrined and Merle looked pissed.

I was to have an armed escort to the bathroom. Fine, two was better than four. I turned to head down the stairs once I hit the first landing and turned ninety degrees to go down I would be able to make out the huddled form of the fifth holdout right where I had tossed him. My two compadres were well behind me and my bulk would ensure that they would not spot him as we descended, but a moment of action was close. As long as it wasn't Fred, that was good, he seemed like the type that could shoot the wings off a fly while galloping on horse back.

This was not going to be easy. Merle was first behind me but he was getting too close and dammit if I couldn't almost feel the muzzle of the barrel pointed at my back. Could I take a hit in the back? I mean if he severed my spine would Hugh be able to do anything to get me upright again, especially in the few moments it would take for him to do anything.

I descended the stairs my brain working feverishly to come up with something that didn't involve me lying in a pool of my own filth as opposed to wearing it. I got to the first landing, I don't know if the moon was rising in the sky or Anna had lit some candles but the lower floor had more light than I remember and my last edible tidbit was clearly visible from where I stood. "Hey, there's something down here," I said looking back at Merle.

"Well, what is it?" he asked with concern.

"How the hell should I know?" I told him.

"Go check it out," he motioned with his gun.

"No way, man. I don't even have a gun," I told him.

"What the hell is the hold up?" Charlie asked Merle as he caught up.

"Fuckin' clown says there's something down at the bottom of the stairs."

"Well, go check it out," Charlie told me over Merle's shoulder.

"He says he's not gonna because he doesn't have a gun," Merle answered for me.

"As big as you are and you're a chicken?" Charlie asked with malice.

"Fuck you. You have a gun and I don't see you in any rush to go see what it is," I snarled.

"Who's missing from upstairs?" Charlie was asking more of himself than Merle.

"I haven't seen Ben for hours and Red, I don't know I was dozing off. You think they're pulling a train on that Anna chick because I'd like to get in on some of that," Merle sneered.

"Yeah, end of the world and Sister Anna wanted to go out with a bang," Charlie said mockingly.

'A nun?' I thought. God, that sounded so tasty, so fresh. Her meat was going to be so sweet!

'Hungry!' Hugh demanded.

'Me too, little buddy!' I told him.

I could see the equations working in Charlie's head. Do I give the clown a gun or do I go past him and see what is causing this traffic jam. Both had inherent dangers built in, so he did the next best thing. "Merle, go check it out."

Merle was about to protest.

"Girls, what the hell is the problem!" Fred yelled down in a loud whisper but with force.

Merle talked first hoping to get his point across. "Fucking clown says there's something downstairs but the pasty pansy won't go check it out because he says he doesn't have a gun and Charlie said I should do it instead, but I don't want to go past the freak."

"Is it moving?" Fred asked. I shook my head and Merle relayed the message.

"Tell the clown to do it or you'll shoot him," Fred said.

I couldn't see Fred from this vantage point but I wanted to make sure he heard me. "Not very Christian-like," I told him.

"You're not in any immediate danger if it isn't moving, so now I'm curious as to what it is and how it got there," Fred said.

"So hungry!" I yelled inadvertently. I placed my hands over my mouth like I was a demure woman who had just loudly belched in a high priced restaurant.

"What did you just say?" Charlie asked.

"He said he was 'so hungry'," Merle said.

"I know what the hell he said dipshit," Charlie said. "I'm just wondering why."

"Charlie, what the hell is going on?" Fred asked.

Charlie turned to answer as did the ever intrusive Merle. 'Now or never'. I sprung from the landing like a flea to a delectable dog thigh. Charlie must have sensed something because he was turning back around. Merle was oblivious. Charlie's gun was coming up to a firing position but unless he was going to blow a hole in Merle to get to me I was going to be just fine.

Charlie's eyes widened as I narrowed the gap.

"Fuck me!" Fred said as he watched me crash into Merle and Charlie. I'm pretty sure I snapped a few of Charlie's ribs as our combined weights plunged into his side and he impacted with heavy wooden stairs. Merle was still clueless, air was whooshing from Charlie's mouth as his punctured lung collapsed.

Friendly fire be damned, Fred started popping off rounds, at least two of which caught me in the shoulder. I pulled my prize up into a bear hug and retreated back down the stairs. Fred didn't stop shooting, prematurely ending Charlie's suffering with a bullet to the head. Merle was full on screaming as Charlie's brain matter cascaded down his face.

"You fucked up my supper Fred," I yelled.

"What are you?" Fred yelled, placing two more shots into the landing wall I had already vacated making the turn so that I could eat in peace.

"Ch-Ch-Charlie's dead," Merle said the gun in his hand completely forgotten as he slipped into shock.

"And so are you," I told him as I ripped his mouth off. His dry and cracked lips tasted a lot like beef jerky. Merle was still screaming but it was muted with the blood from his lipless face running into the back of his throat. I wanted him to stay alive as long as possible, living meat tasted so much better.

"Tastes like chicken wings," I told Merle as I stripped the meager meat from his fingers. Merle passed out. Too bad I was going to miss his dinner conversation. I laughed as I bit through the base of his thumb. "Damn, it even looks like a drum stick," I said holding it up to the moonlight spilling through the stained glass window.

Anna was a few feet away from me, watching the entire event. "Want some?" I asked, holding up a fat big toe. Merle had some abnormally large toes. The fungus under the toe nails added a tanginess I found pleasing. Anna waved her hands back and forth.

"How could you?" she asked.

I began to rip large strands of skin from Merle's legs. I was going to skin him alive. I had read once that the Japanese used to do this to their prisoners because they would live longer as opposed to taking it from the arms first.

"I'm hungry," I told her as if this was the most normal answer to her question. Merle was moaning in his passed out state for that I was immensely pleased. I quickly ripped his sweat pants off as they got in the way of my eating, I thanked him for his consideration. Sweat pants were way easier to shred than blue jeans.

"Commando. Very brave," I told him, although what he was packing wasn't much larger than a cocktail wienie. I would save that for later, kind of like an after dinner mint. I pulled a strip clean from the top of Merle's foot to half way up his abdomen. I was licking my lips as I began to stuff it into my mouth. Anna gagged. "A little hairier than I would have liked but delicious all the same," I told her as I over exaggeratedly licked my fingers. "Oh come on," I told her as she stood there with her horrified expression. "I'm only doing what all of God's creatures do."

She looked aghast that I would invoke his name. "You are not a creature of God. You are an abomination."

"Be that as it may," I said before plunging down into Merle's mid section ripping his outie belly button free from its moorings. I chewed it a few times before responding. "Sorry, I don't like to talk with my mouth full. Manners and all." I grinned. She paled. "But Sister, didn't you just earlier make a deal with this abomination?"

Anna looked mortified that I had found out her calling. It was one thing to be ashamed of your deeds. It was a whole other animal to let down your maker.

"It's alright Sister, that's another of God's instincts instilled into His creatures—self preservation. You cannot judge me any differently when you yourself have placed your well-being above that of others. I don't have a problem with your lack of altruism although because of it I question your career choice. Something more like a tax collector or a politician seems like it would have been more up your alley."

"I'm nothing like you!" she screamed.

"Whatever," I said. I didn't really care as I ripped Merle's left nipple off. Tough bastard, he looked like he was contemplating coming to. "You should probably stay asleep friend because this is going to hurt like hell," I told him right before I ripped his right nipple off to match the other side.

"Anna, what the hell is going on down there?" Fred asked. I could tell he was warring with himself, worry over the fate of the Sister that had sold him out or his own personal safety.

I looked Anna in the eye. "You know he's going to come down here and see if he can help."

She nodded dejectedly.

"You could save him."

"I could?" she asked with a small glimmer of hope.

"Yes, warn him not to come down, but I'm still famished; I have to eat someone," I told her. My blood soaked teeth glistened as I smiled.

"I'm coming down, Anna," Fred cried out. "Just tell me what's going on."

"Fred, what the hell are you doing?" Zak said. "You can't go down there. I'll be alone."

"Then come with me," Fred said.

I could hear Fred trying to come down the stairs as quietly as possible, but the creaking stairs were betraying his every movement.

Zak had made up his mind. I did not hear two sets of feet descending.

'Divide and conquer.' Before I stood I tore Merle's patella free, gelatinous goo hung from it which I greedily slurped up.

"Anna, what was that?" Fred asked, stopping his downward movement.

"Last chance," I told Anna as I stood. She turned away. "That's my good girl. God doesn't give a shit about those idiots with hero syndrome. He cares about survivors. He cares about those who will do all in their power to preserve the gift of life, the gift that he has given to us all. Not those assholes that would throw it all away by running into a burning building or jumping on a grenade." I crept quietly over to the bottom of the stairs as Anna cried softly.

"Sister... Merle, are you alright?" Fred asked quietly from the first landing. "I'm going to drill a hole in your head, clown!" Fred shouted. I think he was more trying to convince himself that he wasn't scared than actually feel like he was intimidating me. Maybe next he would start to whistle, although I never knew the logic behind that stupid move. If you were in a building or a home and you weren't entirely sure if you were alone, why would you announce your damn self? Maybe it was to mask the noise of the boogeyman's approach as he plunged your own kitchen knife through your kidney.

I was at the bottom of the stairs hidden by the wall. Anna had walked farther away, not wanting to witness the ensuing action and maybe if Fred did somehow kill me she would now have plausible deniability that she knew where I was.

'Oh not now!' I stood bolt upright, my sphincter loosening completely. Feces blew through like a stiff breeze through a tunnel, sure a shit-caked tunnel but you get the idea. I used to think cooking liver and onions was the worst smell this planet had to offer, that wasn't even close. I can't imagine flies would even be drawn to what was leaking from my anus.

Fred was gagging violently from the first landing. It was a good thing too because I was locked in this position, I bet stupid Hugh couldn't even chew a tongue and walk at the same time. Fred started blasting holes in the wall near where I was standing.

'Hugh, this might be a good time to wrap up,' I begged my besieger.

The speed with which Hugh released control caught me completely off guard. I collapsed to the floor. This saved our lives as Fred shot two huge holes about head high right where I had been.

"That was close, Fred!" I yelled, laughing.

"You're a sick clown—let me put you out of your misery!" Fred yelled back. I could hear him placing shells into the rifle. I didn't think I could get up and make it to him before he was ready to fire again and if I remembered correctly, he was also wearing a sidearm, so that would be a bad move all around.

"Killing me, Fred, would put me out of *your* misery," I stressed.

"What have you done with the Sister? Don't you have any sanctity for the Cloth?" Fred cried.

"Only when it gets stuck in my teeth," I mocked, crawling away from his firing zone.

"Where is Merle?" Fred demanded.

"Halfway through my colon, I would imagine," I answered.

Fred began anew with the wall drilling holes. I waited until he ran out.

"Fred-Fred-Fred, what would Jesus think of you tearing up his home?" I asked.

Fred began to drive bullets back into his gun, shit how many of the damn things did he have? I've gotta eat—Hugh is a growing boy. I laughed at my own joke. I was still on my hands and knees when I looked over to the battered body of Merle, still clutching his pistol, looked like a Glock but I couldn't be sure, never had much use for them.

'Can zombies use guns?' I asked Hugh.

'Zombie? Hungry.'

'Something new and unusual my tapewormie friend.'

I half crawled excitedly over to Merle, and reached for the gun. I could move my fingers but it was difficult almost like they were wrapped together with duct tape. At first I looked like I was trying to paw the gun from him, my hand was moving as one whole unit as opposed to five separate parts. I had to concentrate hard to move each digit independent of the other. The problem arose when I moved on to the next finger the previous one would revert to something akin to a claw pose. "How fucking cliché," I told Merle. "A zombie with claw hands."

A fresh volley of rounds broke through the silence, Fred's shots were eerily close. 'Dumbass.' He must have heard me talking. The one good thing about a claw hand was that it closely resembled the way my hand would look if I was holding a gun. I managed to finally wrap my left hand around it, which was funny considering I'm a righty, but it was the easier of the two to work with. Now how long was it going to take to send the trigger pull thought to my finger and then have it react? That was the million dollar question.

Anna was watching my every move, I could hear Fred going back upstairs, probably for more rounds or his nerve had finally broke. I stood up thrusting the small pistol jerkily away from my body.

"How's that for a nightmare, Sister? A zombie with a gun. Scares the hell out of me and I'm the one doing it." I laughed. Anna was crying now. "Oh I'm sorry did I upset you, I shouldn't have used the H E double hockey sticks word in the house of the Lord." And then I couldn't help it, I full on laughed, the sound of it reverberating throughout the entire quiet church. Anna shrunk down into herself. Not a peep from Fred or Zak; I didn't blame either one.

"I'm ready to give myself up!" I yelled to Fred, my gaze fixed tightly on the hand holding the gun.

Anna said, "No," softly.

"You say something, sweetheart?" I shifted my gaze toward her.

'Eat it!' Hugh demanded.

"It', Hugh? She is one of the most perfect specimens I have ever seen in my life. I wish I could fuck her before I ate her. Shit, Hugh, Anna there is fine dining at its best. Merle, in comparison, was like eating at Chuck E Cheese. No, we're going to savor every tasty morsel.' I must have been salivating excessively because drool was pooling at my feet. This did not go unnoticed by Anna, although she did not move. Where was she going to go?

"Why don't you come upstairs, clown, and receive your salvation!" Fred yelled.

"I'd like to, Fred, I really would, but it seems I've busted up my leg something fierce in the fall. You're going to have to come down and administer the justice I so desperately need and want."

"Well, you've got to know I don't believe you, clown."

"It's Hugh, dammit!" I yelled. "I... I mean Timothy," I said with much less force.

"Oh, that's rich." Fred yelled down. "A psychotic clown with an associative disorder. Or is it dissociative?"

"You asking me?" Zak asked. "I don't even have a clue what the hell you're talking about."

"Fuck you, Fred!" I screamed. "How about this then? Get your sweet ass over here," I said to Anna. Her head was shaking so violently back and forth I thought she was going to break her damn neck. "If I have to come over there and get you I might just take me a little bite for the effort."

She was moving, it was reluctantly and slower than it should have been but she was coming my way.

"What are you doing, *clown*?" Fred emphasized the moniker.

He was taunting me but there was also a tremor in his voice as he realized I might have something that could force his hand.

"Say hello to the nice dead man upstairs," I told Anna. I grabbed the top of her head to stop its to and fro movement. She squirmed under the contact some viscous fluid dripped down from my hand to her forehead she crossed her eyes in a vain attempt to possibly garner its contents. It was of my belief that she would be better off not knowing.

"Fred, help me." Anna whimpered, it was exactly what I needed her to say but she didn't do it for my benefit, sister or not she was no Mother Teresa.

I bent down and licked her ear, stopping long enough to probe her ear canal with the tip of my tongue. Her quaking stopped, replaced by rigidity a plank of wood would be proud of. The pressure must have compressed her bladder.

"Ah, the smell of warm piss in the night, it's like a little slice of Heaven. Don't you think?" I whispered in her ear.

"If you hurt her, I'll kill you, clown!" Fred yelled.

"Really, Fred, you don't have anything more original than that?" I pinched Anna's shoulder until she squealed in pain.

Fred ran down three steps before Zak's words stopped him. "It's a damn trap. Fred, you can't be that stupid."

"I know it's a trap, what the hell else am I supposed to do?" Fred answered him.

"Live," Zak told him.

"See, Zak gets it," I said softly to Anna. "Not Fred, though. Oh, he'll be down here lickety-split."

'HUNGRY!' Hugh screamed in protest.

"SHUT THE FUCK UP, HUGH!!! We'll eat when I god damn say its time to eat!"

Anna let loose with another volley of urine.

"Damn, did I say that out loud?" I asked the quiet room. I was answered by my own echo. If I hadn't already crossed the line to Crazy Town, I was rapidly approaching and there were no stops between here and there. At least Hugh had taken a back seat for the moment. "That's right, I'm in charge here!" I yelled, I could have been talking about the church or my body. Both would have been correct.

"Losing, it clown? Why don't you do us all a favor and go to the altar and fall on a sword or something?" Fred said.

I would swear he was on the first landing now. If the dipshit had just shut up he probably could have just snuck up on me during my psychotic episode. Is that what I'm calling it now? I moved Anna so that when Fred came down she would be in front of me. Although that was like trying to hide an airplane behind a Volkswagen. I couldn't imagine Fred taking the shot and harming her, though.

Fred came down the remainder of the stairs quickly scanning the room with his rifle. The barrel came to rest on us and if I wasn't mistaken, my head. I ducked down a bit and the muzzle followed. Still, he didn't fire.

"Why don't you come out from behind the lady and we'll settle this like men?" Fred said.

"How about you put your rifle down first? Hardly seems fair, you with a firearm and all and me with just my teeth."

"What are you, clown?"

I could tell he was genuinely interested, not just trying to get a rise out of me. I didn't quite know what to tell him, so I didn't answer.

"You put down the rifle, I'll let the Sister go," I said as I blew snot out of my nose almost completely covering the top of her head. She most likely would have fainted to the ground if I wasn't holding her up.

Fred took a step toward me. "Far enough, Fred. The church was diffused with darkness but Fred's trigger knuckle shone a bright white as he kept six and a half pounds of pressure on a seven pound trigger. "You know you could always just blow a few of those cannon rounds through little missy here to get to me." As quickly as I said it, Fred seemed to contemplate it and reject it. "Well, what is it going to be Fred—the girl for your rifle and then we can settle this like men?"

'If I still am a man,' a distant thought rang out.

Fred was easily double my age and half my size but the crazy bastard still put his rifle to the side. "Alright, I've done my part," he said, holding his hands up to prove he hadn't concealed anything.

"Move away from it, Fred," I said calmly. He did as I asked and I laid the passed-out Anna down gently. It wasn't that I cared a shit for her safety, I just didn't want to bruise my meat. I stood to my full height; the wide eyed stare from Fred let me know that he instantly regretted his decision and his gaze kept shifting towards his now discarded rifle, my guess was in an attempt to see how quickly he could get to it. "A deal's a deal, Fred. Or would you renege in the house of the Lord?"

"Let's do this," Fred said, trying to psyche himself up.

I raised my gun-toting left hand up, the barrel shone a dull blue. "What the fu—" Were Fred's final words as my trigger finger obediently obeyed and three times no less. I impressed myself with my grouping, the first shot caught him square in the Adam's apple and before he could even react I placed another in the bottom half of his jaw and the third ripped open the top of his face, but to be fair he was dropping fast, it wasn't that my point of aim had wavered.

"Did you kill the fucker?" Zak asked from atop the stairs.

"Why yes, Zak. Indeed I did," I replied as I approached Fred's still jerking body. At some point Anna had come up to my side and was looking down at Fred. She was murmuring something, could have been the Lord's prayer or a peanut butter cookie recipe, I didn't really give a shit either way. Hugh wanted to eat Fred but I liked the blood to still be pounding through the veins in my food.

"Oh shit, oh shit," Zak said, close to panicking. "Listen, mister, I don't have a beef with you."

"That's funny that you should word it that way, Zak, because I actually consider you my beef." Wild, unaimed shots rang down the stairwell. I was fairly certain that if I walked slowly up the stairs Zak couldn't hit me, but 'fairly certain' was still a big chance to take when one was dealing with one's life. "Zak, you come down here and give yourself up. I'll make it relatively painless." Well as painless as having your liver ripped free from your still warm body could be, anyway. More wild shots, unless his bullets could make a ninety degree turn I should be fine.

Anna was still murmuring under her breath, an unnoticed Rosary in her hands. So much for the peanut butter cookie recipe theory. She was looking better and better by the minute. My stomach growled so loudly she momentarily stopped her praying and Zak let loose some more bullets. The sound of the loud 'click' as Zak fired the last bullet in his magazine was immediately followed by a loud clatter and an 'Oh Jesus' as what I figured was the empty magazine of Zak's gun fell down the stairs to come resting on the first landing.

'Dinner is served!' I thought as I swept into action. I pushed against the wall as I rounded the corner to get onto the base of the stairs. I was halfway up the first set of stairs before Zak knew what was happening. He was midway down the second set as I rounded the turn on the landing; the surprise of seeing me froze him in indecision, but only for a split second. He reached for a large bowie knife strapped to his hip. I launched up the remaining few steps as he pulled the knife free from its sheath. He brought it up as my mouth opened in anticipation of a meal. The pain was excruciating as the blade caught the edge of my eyeball ripping it clean from its moorings in my orbital socket. For a moment I had the duality vision of looking at Zak's terrified face and the red carpet runner on the stairs; not a pleasant sensation.

I was screaming or maybe it was Hugh, quite possibly both of us. I staggered back and almost fell the three steps back to the landing. Zak had let go of his knife which was stuck in my sliced eyeball, now hanging precariously down to my navel. The weight of the foreign object snapped the optical nerve, sending my eye rolling down the rest of the stairs. My head snapped slightly back as the nerve recoiled back into its socket like an over powered tape measure let go from twelve feet.

I could hear Anna screaming to mimic my own; she must have come across my wayward eyeball. Zak was upstairs rummaging around for something, another weapon most likely. Fire bursting pain in my head or not, I had to get up there and finish him off before he found something to do me in with. Now it was personal.

My left eye socket seared in pain. Hugh was in the background, frantically doing damage control. He would stop the bleeding but we'd never see out of that eye again. I was going to start with Zak's eyes for this! He was at the far corner of the room holding a baseball bat.

"Don't make me use this," he begged, his arms shaking like a vibrator left on an oak nightstand.

"I can't just walk away now, Zak. You took my eye, now I'm going to take yours."

He swung the bat violently even though I was a good fifteen feet away. I slowly approached. Zak backed up even farther but unless he could incorporate himself into the structure of the church he wasn't going anywhere.

"End of the line," I told him evenly.

This was a lesson I wouldn't soon forget. Cornered animals are unpredictable. Zak began screaming as he ran toward me. I had not even enough time to raise my hands up as he swung the bat. My height was the only thing that saved my life as my shoulder caught the brunt of the swing, but even as the bat struck my shoulder and struck the side of my head I could feel my skull break in a couple of places.

'DON'T!' Hugh screamed. 'PAIN,' although this mostly translated as the color Red.

Thick blood poured from the hole in my head. Another shot like that and Zak would be standing over my prone body. My head was reeling, Hugh was screaming and Zak was pressing the attack. He pulled the bat back and struck again, this time I was able to raise my arm up. My forearm splintered as Zak caught it with the fat part of the Louisville Slugger.

"Fuck you!" he spat. "Just fucking die!" He pulled the bat back into the cocked position again.

'Move or die, move or die' kept flashing through my head like a neon sign.

Anna took this the most opportune of times to save my life, even if it was not her intention I appreciated it immensely. Zak hesitated for a millisecond as she came to the door, screaming to know if I was dead, I didn't know she cared, I thought sarcastically.

I moved in biting Zak's left thumb clean off, he dropped the bat as I chewed noisily on the digit. I spit out some bone bits as Zak was hunched over trying to staunch the flow of blood.

"Betcha that fuckin' hurts," I said. He was full on sobbing now, the fight bitten out of him.

"I'm so sorry," Anna kept repeating over and over, but she wasn't willing to come and console him personally.

"That's alright. I forgive you and most likely so will your God," I told her.

She looked up at me with rage in her eyes and then turned to go downstairs.

"God, I'm so hungry," I told Zak as I ripped through his ear. Anna's footfalls were masked by the renewed efforts of Zak's pleas. But just like God, I had turned a deaf ear and a blind eye!

'Pretty fucking witty,' I thought, rending the flesh from his nose. I was really enjoying the elasticity of the cartilage; it made for some serious chewing, reminded me somewhat of jerky. I pulled the white mass that was Zak's nose and dipped in to the wound by his ear. Zak's shoulders were pumping up and down as he sobbed quietly. Shock must have set down deeply into Zak, that was the only reason I could figure why he wasn't fighting back. "Few more minutes, half hour tops and you won't be able to feel a thing," I told him. Zak began to suck on his still present thumb. "Aw, how cute," I told him as I pulled his remaining ear off, first sucking the blood then nibbling the flesh off so that I could get to the chewy center.

'Didn't they do a lollipop commercial eerily similar to this?' I asked Hugh. No response. 'Yeah there was an owl with glasses I think.'

'Eat. Fix,' Hugh replied.

"I get it—you need food to fix all of the injuries our dinner guest inflicted," I said aloud.

Zak was too busy rocking back and forth sucking his thumb to take any more note of the external world.

"Bye, Zak. It's been a pleasure to eat you," I said picking up his discarded bat and smashing his skull so that I would have easier access to his juicy brains. I peeled away the large fragments of splintered skull matted with blood and hair and drove my hand deep into his skull cavity coming up with a large succulent fistful of brain. Warm brains sounding like just about the best damn thing on the planet right now.

I must have passed out or fallen asleep or maybe just went into a deep fugue state as I devoured Zak but by the time I snapped out of it we were down to the bowels of our host and sunshine was streaming in through the windows. My head had stopped leaking, but my eye was never coming back, Hugh hadn't even seen fit to pull the optic nerve all the way in before sealing the wound shut. Now it looked like I had a tapeworm hanging from my face. I was going to have to really step my game up if I ever wanted to get me some again.

It was Anna's screams that got me moving, Hugh wanted to take a legendary dump. I told him he had to wait; he was not enthused but he acquiesced. I ran down the stairs which was cumbersome considering I was carrying another human inside of me but wasn't pregnant, though I was eating for two, I mused. I turned from the stairs, the stupid bitch had unlocked the church doors in a vain attempt to get away from me, did she miss the four or five hundred zombies perched outside that were now streaming in like lost souls clamoring for forgiveness.

Anna was picking her poison as she stumbled back from the flesh worshippers, she turned and ran full speed past me and up the stairs. The zombies were only seconds behind. Dammit, I had never played well with others and I wasn't about to start now. Anna was *my* prize, I had paid dearly for the right to eat her and I'd be damned if I was going to let these slobs spoil it for me. Hugh started a buzzing in my head, I was thinking this was the beginning of his plan to be rid of me. It was an incapacitating sound, I couldn't think—it was all encompassing, I felt like drowning in the hum.

'Well played,' I told him as both my body and my mind fell to our knees. Hugh did not respond, he didn't owe the defeated anything I thought as I rolled over onto my side. 'Just finish it,' I thought, 'I've got no defense for this.'

Funny thing was Hugh wasn't doing anything to me, he was communicating with the zombies in the church. Whatever he was saying it involved telling them to not go up the stairs. The zombies had stopped no more than two or three feet from where I had collapsed, they were looking eagerly at the stairwell but they did not come any closer.

'Eliminate. Eat female,' Hugh said.

'Shit, Hugh, what the hell did you do?' I asked, like usual he didn't answer. I think I could kind of get used to the little guy, he didn't say much but he sure packed a mean punch, I thought as I stood up. I felt the old familiar rigidity coming on, I asked Hugh to stop. Again he listened.

"I just want to do this right," I said aloud. I pulled my clown pants down to my ankles which was no easy feat considering the poundage of shit and human debris stuck to me. I squatted like a germaphobe female in an overflowing port-apottie. I'd never had stage fright before but taking a shit in front of a hundred or so zombies was intimidating. My asshole was puckered tight, until Hugh decided enough was enough, I think a bowling ball would have fit easily once Hugh loosed it. Zak remnants flowed from me like a brown river of mud. The smell was horrific ambrosia. The closest zombies were ankle deep in my offal, it seemed to excite them as they began to sniff enthusiastically. It felt so good it was like having an anal orgasm if such a thing were possible, no matter what I'd told all the girls before that I'd convinced to have that type of sex with, I had never believed in it before now that is.

A few minutes later I was gleefully pulling my pants back up. 'That was thoroughly enjoyable, buddy,' I told Hugh. If this was what having a friend was like I could get used to it. The zombies were watching as I began to go up the stairs but not a one of them broke the invisible barrier Hugh had set up.

'Any chance you could tell me what you did back there?' I asked.

No reply was forthcoming for such a long while I didn't figure one was coming at all and when it did I sure wasn't expecting it.

'Fuck off,' Hugh said.

I stopped ascending the stairs, at first shocked that my friend had turned on me and then to laugh uncontrollably when I realized he had been telling the zombies to 'fuck off' not me.

'That's rich, buddy!' I thought as I wiped a phantom tear away from my empty eye socket. Hugh didn't say anything, but I got the distinct impression that he was pretty pleased with himself.

I traveled the rest of the way up with what I would imagine was a very large smirk plastered across my face, although I'm not sure if anyone could have noticed through the blood and bile on my face. I was not prepared for what greeted me at the top of the step. Instead of cowering in the corner, Anna was in the middle of the room standing naked. My old self quaked with desire; she was sculpted as if from the hand of God himself. I had bedded some beauties through the years and not a one of them could hold a candle to the creature that stood before me. The slight knocking in her knees only made her that much more attractive. Compound that with the fact she was a devout virgin married to Christ and Him not being much into conjugal visits made her fucking perfect.

"I am offering everything of me so that you will not kill me," she said with a slight retching hitch to her words.

"What makes you think, Sister, that I would not just take what I want and discard the rest?"

Her eyes widened in alarm. She moved closer, her breasts swaying enticingly. She was trying to hold her breath and when that didn't work she was filtering air through her nearly closed lips and clenched teeth as if that would do anything.

"I can do things for you that you've never had done," she pleaded.

"Oh, I doubt that," I told her. She seemed fairly practiced for someone of the Cloth and her trimmed pussy hair was making me doubt her professed occupation, but I was not yet ready to shatter the illusion.

She openly gagged as she moved even closer, if she could have turned her head all the way back she would have as she pulled my clown pants down. She added her vomit to the mixture already on my clothes, to her merit she didn't skip a beat. She gasped as she stood back up coming face to face with my one eyed monster.

I laughed at her. "Not much you're going to be able to do with that Sister," I told her as I grabbed the base of my cock, the top half black and barely hanging on. I shook it violently until it dropped to the floor with an audible plop. I was pretty impressed considering that was only about half my penis.

Anna began to vomit anew spewing stomach butter all over my decapitated manhood.

"I'd really like to help you out, *Sister*, I really would, but it looks like that's just not in the cards."

Anna's ploy for life was over and now she knew it. Not that I was ever going to let her live, even as a kid I used to like to play with my food before I ate it.

"How could God let something like you live!" she spat.

"We are the wrath of God!" I answered her harshly.

She must have thought I was talking about the zombie collective when in actuality I meant me and Hugh.

Anna began to back up, searching frantically for anything that resembled a weapon.

"Should I wait a few minutes more and see if you come up with anything?" I asked her mockingly.

Her eyes flared as she looked over to me, and for the second time Anna surprised the hell out of me. She dropped to her knees, hands clasped in front of her, head bowed, she was reciting the Lord's Prayer.

"Get up!" I yelled at her. She was infuriating the hell out of me and I didn't know why. I wanted her to be scared and cowering it just made it that much more enjoyable for me. Maybe the endorphins and adrenaline combined with the meat made it taste better.

I ran up on her, my heavy footfalls causing her to move slightly as the floor yielded to my weight, but she did not look up or stop her prayers.

"Your God will not save you!" I yelled, and still she continued. "Oh, I get it, you're trying to save *me!* Well here's a newsflash—I don't need saving because zombies never die! I'm as right as rain!

Hugh was screaming at me as I turned and walked back down the stairs and through the throng of zombie brethren. They watched as I left the church before they headed up the stairs. Anna never screamed out as she was eaten alive, I stayed on the lawn looking up at the sky. Hugh had finally relented after a solid hour of letting me know how he felt about losing a meal. Zombies began to come back out through the church doors as they must have realized that all the potential food source within had been depleted. Some stood still like me, some headed off, but the majority just kind of milled around aimlessly. With no job, hobby or external obligations there wasn't a whole bunch to do.

I looked at my peers. We were a sad lot; I was missing half my penis and an eye and I was far from the worst. There was one old lady zombie who must have awoken from a deep sleep to realize she had become the undead, she had not had the foresight to put her dentures in, just thinking of the cravings she must be going through hurt my stomach.

'What now, Hugh?' I asked my only friend.

'Eat,' he told me.

And really, what other option was there? I could hear gunshots in the distance, so that meant food was available, but like all great predators it was time to minimize risk to my health, such as it was, and maximize sustenance. The young, the old and the infirm would offer the least resistance and probably the least taste but I couldn't keep taking damage—Hugh could only stitch together so much. A hospital sounded like the most opportune place to ransack, but when the outbreak hit that would be where the first zombies showed up, meaning the larder would likely have been emptied on that first day.

Where next and then it struck like a bolt of lightning—nursing home! There was the Saint Vincent Home for the Aged on my way to work, I never gave it more than a passing glance but right now it sounded like a twenty-four hour Wendy's. The food was way past prime but the fight would be long gone from those inhabitants. I began to whistle as I walked straight down the center line of the empty roadway. A zombie or two looked my way because of the unnatural noise I emitted but none investigated any further. I avoided any street where I could hear fighting, most times it involved voracious gun fire followed almost immediately by screaming. Fifty zombies would fall for every human eaten and still we would win, but then what? When man became extinct what became of us? I shuddered to think of our potential demise and pushed it from my mind as I concentrated on getting us intact to St. Vincent's.

There were zombies already congregated around the nursing home, which meant food was still available, and none of them were being shot another plus.

'Hugh, I'm going to find us a way in, can you tell the others to 'fuck off' again?'

The buzz started at the base of my skull, I ran around to the back of the nursing home a gated fence my only hindrance had stopped the others in their tracks.

'Stop, Hugh!' I begged, just able to shut the gate behind me before the blinding pain of Hugh's communication threatened to overwhelm me.

I rested my head against the cool steel chain links as I waited for the tide of pain to peel back. It was slow like the outgoing tide and it was long moments before I could stand completely back up, I was going to have to be very careful before I told him to do that. I had been ready for this one and it had hurt twice as much, what could I expect the next time? Zombies bowed the fence in where they made contact but they were more likely to become pressed through like Play-doh through a mold than be able to follow me. A large black man dressed in a white orderly uniform came up behind me as I went to the back entrance.

'Fuck off?' Hugh was asking me if he should tell the other zombie to go screw.

'No, no, no!' I begged. 'I'll take care of it.'

I swept the big man's legs out from under him, after he had fallen I got behind him and put my right arm around his throat, and then grabbed my right wrist with my left hand. The loud crack as I snapped his neck sent a crow flying from a nearby tree.

'He won't bother us anymore,' I told Hugh.

As I got up and stepped away the orderly got to his feet.

"Wasn't expecting that."

The orderly's head was bent all the way back so that he was staring at me upside down. He kept turning his body to follow his line of sight. I hadn't killed him like I had intended but he was effectively out of commission. An ancient woman looked at me through the large French doors. How could she have possibly flown under Death's radar for so long? I looked better than her. She had wrinkles as deep as fast water carved crevices, her face might look like a mini diorama of the Grand Canyon but her eyes, they were full of intelligence. No jelly-brain there as she watched me dispatch of the orderly. I wasn't the cavalry that she might have been hoping for. She looked down to the lock to make sure it was engaged before she did the unthinkable, she flipped me off.

I stopped to place my hands on my knees as I bent over laughing. There was a good chance I would save the old bird for last just for that. Who knows she might even die from natural causes before I got to her.

I stood up, the laughing felt great but now I was hungry. I walked a few steps around the yard until I found what I was looking for. I motioned for the old biddy to get out of the way as I hefted the rock in my hand, positioning it just right so that I could get maximum velocity before I hurled it at the mostly glass doorway. The lady glared at me but she moved all the same. The crash of glass was a satisfying feeling as large shards shattered to the ground.

"Have you no respect for your elders?" The old crow asked me as I broke through the door, sustaining a few more cuts along the way.

"Only in so far as I can eat one," I told her. It really made no sense but my hunger was beginning to crowd out all higher thought.

There was a man nearly as ancient as the redwoods sitting in a chair, watching a static laced television. "TV dinner." I moved on the unsuspecting victim, odds were he had no clue who he was much less that the world had been basically turned on its ear.

I was directly behind him just as the first impact hit. Old crow had followed me and had the strength to smack me with her cane, she truly was an impressive specimen. She looked five years dead, yet she defended the castle.

"Listen, granny." I turned, doing my best evil stare to make her go shuffling into the night. "I have no issue with you, I plan on eating you eventually, but if you leave me the fuck alone I'll make sure you're last."

"If I was your granny, I would have killed you in your cradle, you atrocity," she shot back, right before she whacked me again.

She would have had a hard time killing a fly with the power behind her swat but she was pissing me off to no end. "Why don't you leave me alone!" She swatted me again, her cane making contact with my exposed optic nerve. I stood to my full height and turned toward her. "That hurt, bitch." I backhanded her across the room. Her dentures went flying and the snap of the impact let me know I had effectively disabled the broad, she lay there in a heap, her ancient hip most likely fractured. She never did cry out and she watched as I ate my TV dinner. And like most of those meals, it tasted like shit He was stringy, gamey and tasted like wet fungus, but none of that stopped me.

The old crow looked a little worse for wear; either the pain or watching her friend get eaten was having an effect. "I'll be back," I told her as I went down the hallway, looking for more food to round out my dinner.

"Meals on wheels!" I shouted, another old lady was crouched down in a wheel chair she was mumbling something incoherent as I grabbed the back of her chariot to spin her around. I wanted to get a good look at her before I ate.

"Howdy Doody!" she exclaimed, clapping her hands together excitedly.

At first I thought she was greeting me and then I realized she had me confused with that Alfred E. Newman lookalike. I have no idea why that irked the hell out of me. I hated being a clown. I punched her so hard in the face her chair kept rolling until it banged off the far wall close to thirty feet away. She was most certainly dead. "Dumb ass," I scolded myself. I had just wasted food and it was in diminishing supply.

I made short work of that hallway, a good portion of the residents had perished when the staff either took off to be with their own families or were turned like the orderly on the lawn. There were four old ladies and one man on his last legs, the oxygen tank sustaining him nearly dry. The hunger was abated for the moment but the meager meat these people provided would not stave it off for long. It prowled like a living animal in the periphery of my mind. I needed to distract myself from this constant in my life, I had at once simplified and complicated my life these last few days. The ever present pursuit of pussy had merely turned into a different addiction. I had no moral dilemma with the passing of others by my own hand so that I could live. The issue arose when my food fought back, how much nursing home food could I eat?

I strode back down the hallway, long wet glistening entrails dragging behind me, I had stepped in one of my victim's innards and it had stuck to my shoe. I pulled what remained of my TV dinner out of his chair and sat down heavily. The chair creaked from my added bulk but held fast, I spun it so I was directly facing Old Crow.

Her eyes were half closed and she was breathing quickly and shallowly.

"Must hurt," I mimicked a tone of empathy.

Her eyes opened slowly. "I've had seven children, I've felt worse pain."

"Seven kids and yet they all still deposited you in here to die. Kind of ungrateful, I'd say."

She did not respond to my barb. "What are you? You can't be one of those things. They don't talk. Are you just a sick human who's finally come into his true calling?"

'What exactly am I?' I thought. I had been human once, before Hugh came along, but then he had been running the show so all I could do was watch as he performed every imaginable perversion. But I had slowly taken the reins back and now I was running the machine, so what did that make me? I was infinitely more of a monster than Hugh. He was only doing what his instinct was telling him to do. I could have put a bullet in my head before he ever had the chance to stop me.

"Fuck you!" I screamed at Old Crow shooting out of my chair.

"Strike a nerve, did I?" she snorted softly.

I stormed down the corridor, looking for another wing I had yet to plunder. I ate the first thing I came across, it smelled like old cabbage and tasted worse. I was so upset I had completely ignored Hugh's warnings that thing I had eaten was already dead.

'Bad!' Hugh lamented.

'Who cares—food is food!' I yelled back at him.

'More me!' Hugh shot back.

'That makes no sense! I'm hungry!' I told Hugh, then I stopped. I was the monster Old Crow had flat out said that I was. It wasn't Hugh who had told me I was famished it was me. I was a self-aware zombie; didn't that put me right up there with werewolves and vampires?

"Maybe even the boogeyman," I said with no little amount of glee. I was becoming a legend—who wouldn't be pleased with that?

I strode back down to where Old Crow lay. "I am a monster you hag, I am *the* monster!" I shouted proudly. "Never before and never again will there be anything as scary as me. When things go bump in the night children will pray to an empty God that it isn't me!" Old Crow was looking at me with a slight upward pull on the left side of her face giving her the look that she was sneering at me. "I'll rip your face off bitch!" I yelled running over to her. Her head bouncing off the ground as my heavy footfalls caused minor earthquakes on the floor. I started to laugh—it wasn't a comforting 'this is funny' laugh it was a 'trying to hold on to sanity and failing miserably' laugh. Old Crow was dead and she looked like she had got the last laugh. I kicked her in the head, her body slid across the highly waxed floor to come to a rest against the far wall, the delicate bones in her decrepit face all shattered. I lost my balance as my plant foot slipped from under me, my ass struck first followed by the whiplash movement of my head as I struck the floor.

"Who the *fuck* waxes the floor in an old age home? Must be the hip replacement companies," I mused as I sat up. Old Crow wasn't looking at me anymore, although that would have been tough considering her face was now recessed into her brain cavity.

'Trouble!' Hugh shouted.

I scanned my immediate surroundings, and kept as silent as possible trying to ascertain what danger Hugh was seeing. I tried to ask him for clarification but in typically Hugh fashion he was ignoring me. "Fuck you too, Hugh, I don't need you either!"

"I'm sick of eating this trash! I am Timothy and I will eat what I want!" I shouted as I pushed open the front doors to the home, zombies streamed past me to get into the place, still must have been some residents left. I pushed zombies out of my way much as I had done to defensive linemen on the football field. The mindless cretins never had the presence of mind to get out of my way; I sent at least three of them to whoever their maker may have been.

I had no sooner cleared the throng when I heard the hum of a car engine idling. I walked up the street a few feet as the zombies cleared from the roadway. It wasn't difficult to ascertain where the noise was coming from as exhaust streamed from beneath a mostly closed garage door. There was a good chance whoever was trying to off themselves wasn't making a very good go of it. With the garage door as open as it was, there was more than better odds they were still alive. Perfect, I'd always loved smoked meat!

As I approached the door I thought about using a catchy catchphrase, but 'I'm back' or 'here's Johnny' seemed so cliché. Maybe something a little less well known like 'Hey Georgie, want your boat?' but that really didn't make much sense. Something would come to me. I reached down to pull the door up but it held fast, the electric opener must have been engaged. I pulled harder, the door began to buckle under the stress.

"Cheap ass aluminum!" I roared as I stood tall, the handle had sheared off in my hand but there was at least a two foot gap between the driveway and the bottom of the door now. I was not at all happy about having to degrade myself by crawling for my food, but the old biddies had done little to quench my hunger. I needed a more substantial meal and who was I kidding, I was covered in the feces of multiple victims. Smoke poured through the opening, making it difficult to see. I bumped my head on the front end of a large SUV, the familiar blue and white layout of the Beemer logo stared back at me as I rose.

'Nice car' flashed across my head for a second but of more importance was the family of four and the dog still seated packaged neatly for safe transport.

'How thoughtful,' I thought as I removed the father's seatbelt, no extraneous bruising. I unceremoniously dropped him to the ground, he stirred slightly. My spirits soared, he at least was alive, I turned the ignition to the off position to make sure none of my other food stocks expired.

In the passenger seat, the small brunette's lids were semi-opened, the frosted glaze to her eyes gave me the impression she had moved on, at least until I saw her lips moving. She was in a full throated silent scream as I got to within a few inches from her face. Her hands came slightly off her lap in a useless defensive posture.

"It's okay," I told her. "This will only hurt a lot."

"Babies… no… alone," she said weakly through a tortured windpipe.

"What, you don't want me to eat your babies?" I laughed. I turned to look in the back seat. A boy of about seven had long since made his final journey. I reached back and ripped him out of his seat by the neck. His mother was trying in desperation to resuscitate herself enough to help. "You talking about him?" I asked, shaking the boy violently in front of her face. She nodded in resignation.

"Well, you see this piece of shit is already dead," I told her as I repeatedly slammed his head against the dashboard and the windshield, blood spread across the spidery veins his skull had caused in the glass. Mom had tears streaking down her face. "Sucks for him," I told her as I threw him out the car to drop onto his father.

I turned back to see what other treasures I might find. The mom had finally garnered enough strength to place a hand on my arm. I pulled it up to my face and ripped three of her fingers off. I broke at least two of my teeth as I attempted to chew through her wedding ring.

"Bitch!" I yelled as I backhanded her so hard her head smacked against the dashboard to rebound back into the plush headrest, she was once again out cold. 'Pity' I thought it had been kind of fun having her watch, I had never much been into the whole voyeurism thing but it excited me in a way I had not been prepared for.

I watched mom for a few more seconds to see if she was playing possum. I turned in time to see Sparky the family Golden Retriever launch himself at my throat. Got pretty damn close too, if I had not got my right arm up in time he would have taken a significant chunk out of me. My arm burned where his canines had sunk into, fabric tore as he shook his head, trying to do as much damage possible. I slammed my arm down onto the console, but the dog would not let go. He must have some pit bull in him somewhere. I kept bringing my arm down with more and more force until I heard his lower jaw crack, his high pitched whine tore at my nerves. I grabbed him by the scruff and smashed him into the windshield much like I had the boy, their blood now intermingling as the mutt finally lay still in my hand. I threw him onto the meat pile.

"Any more surprises?" I intoned. And there was. "Danielle?" A sixteen or seventeen year old raven-haired beauty slept in the back seat. "But how could that be, that was at least twelve years ago."

***

I had been a sophomore in high school and already considered a major player on the field and off when she had transferred from Pennsylvania. When she had walked into that Biology class that first day I knew I had to have her. I told my lab partner to take a hike before Mr. Cook could assign her to someone else.

"I've got a spot," I told Cook, as I shoved my previous partner Peter Pender away hard enough that he fell to the floor. Cook was not amused but if he didn't do what I asked he would have to deal with Coach Bartlett, and nobody wanted to be on the short end of that stick. Plus Cook loved football, so it wasn't that big a sacrifice for him.

"There you go, Miss?"

"Danielle Hoegler," the angel replied.

"There you go, Danielle. Tim will be your lab partner."

She smiled shyly at me and came over to our station. I swept Pete's things onto the floor to make room. I was so entranced by her I didn't even hear the little nerd cursing at me as his books rained down upon him.

"Pete, shut the hell up," one of his friends begged. "He'll eat you if you keep talking."

"Sorry," Danielle told Pete as she stepped over his belongings.

And that was the beginning of our relationship. We went out for close to nine months, that's about eternity for a high school kid. I was head over heels for her and we had not gotten past any heavy petting. It was Donna Sorji that had fucked everything up for me, she was the town pump and nine months of fondling Danielle and nothing else had my balls scrunched up into twisted blue melons. It was a Friday night. Danielle and her parents were going to see a movie, they had invited me but hanging out with my girl's folks didn't sound like a great time and besides, there was supposed to be a rager of a party. Danielle and I made plans to hook up the following night. The party was everything it had been cracked up to be. There was plenty of beer, the music was loud and I was kicking ass at quarters. For two straight hours I dominated the drinking game before my bladder finally rebelled, I stumbled away excusing myself as I bumped into someone sending them flying into the kitchen cabinets, I hoped they weren't hurt but I didn't stop to check; I was wasted and I needed sweet release.

The line at the downstairs bathroom was eight people deep. Why I didn't just go outside eludes me to this day. I instead found my way to the stairs, a couple of the doors were closed and I could hear the tell-tale moans of those in the throes of orgasm, I normally would have jumped into the doorway and pulled a major coitus interruptus but I could almost taste piss in my throat I was so full of it. I walked into the master bedroom which was thankfully empty and opened the bathroom door.

"Aw fuckin' shit," I said as I was fumbling with my zipper to pull my dick out. Donna was sitting on the vanity smoking a cigarette. "You about done?" I asked her, trying to stuff it back in my pants, the added pressure causing me to squirm.

"Don't mind me," she said puffing away. "Unless you have stage fright."

I had stopped listening the second she said she didn't care. I pulled my buddy back out of my pants, it seemingly weighed a couple of pounds from the added fluid. I arched my back and let loose, the sweet release was invigorating. Donna had hopped down and was now standing next to me as I went.

"What the fuck are you doing?" I asked her, more than a little peeved that she was ruining this religious experience.

"That's a nice cock, what else can it do?" she asked lustily.

"Go away," I told her.

"I know you're going out with Sandra Dee. Her legs are tied together at the knees, have you even felt her tits yet?"

"Fuck off, Donna and let me piss," If I didn't have one hand around my manhood and the other braced against the wall keeping me standing, I would have pushed her away.

"Listen, no one needs to know. I want it and you need it. Fuck, Tim your balls are so blue it looks like you've been storing them in a freezer." She laughed. "And it does look like you're interested." She was looking at my burgeoning penis.

Donna was a slut, no argument there, but she was hot and I was a high school kid. Of course I was getting hard. "No one finds out Donna. I'll fuck you up if this gets back to Danielle."

"Scout's honor," she said as she placed her two closed fingers to her mouth and kissed them. As I finally and blissfully finished up one basic human need, I went for a second one. She closed the toilet seat and sat down on the lid. Luckily the bathroom wasn't too big; as I spread out my arms, bracing myself against two walls. Donna's ministrations were in a word, fantastic. I'd always believed my coach when he said practice makes perfect, and she'd sure had her share. I was close to coming when I heard someone enter into the bedroom but unless it was the President I didn't give a shit and even then he'd have to wait until I was done.

"Tim?" I heard from the open bathroom door.

"Oh—oh *fuck!*" I shouted as I came. Donna had pulled away at that moment, my baby batter arced out and splashed onto her hair and the toilet.

"Oops," Donna said. "Probably should have shut the door."

"How... how could you?" Danielle cried, her eyes huge, taking in this ultimate betrayal.

"Wait, wait. This isn't what it looks like," I said as I pulled my rapidly diminishing cock from Donna's hand and tried to chase her. But she was much smaller and had not been drinking, by the time I bumbled my way down the stairs and through the throng of partygoers she was long gone. She would not accept my phone calls and did not show up to school for the entire school week.

I'd had enough. I was going to wait outside her house until she talked to me, eventually she would have to. I was wholly unprepared for what I witnessed when I went to her house that Friday after school. Two police cruisers were on her front lawn and an ambulance was in the driveway. Mrs. Hoegler was sobbing and she was wrapped up tight in Mr. Hoegler's arms.

Someone was being wheeled out on a gurney, the sheet was pulled up past the face so I couldn't see who it was. It couldn't have been much of an emergency, the men weren't hurrying and the lights to the ambulance weren't even on. Maybe Grandma Hoegler had died, but in all the time we had dated Danielle had never said anything about her. And then the slow dim evil light of dawning came upon me. It started out as a peach pit in my stomach to become a raging alien within me in a matter of moments. The hammering in my chest did little to quell the boiling acid in my stomach, my head felt feverish, my feet were rooted to their spot by the curb.

"Get out of here!" Mr. Hoegler was screaming from his front porch. "You've done enough already, you bastard!" Rage issued forth from every fiber of his being and I had yet to figure out who he was directing his diatribe to.

A cop was heading my way, another was trying to calm Mr. Hoegler down. "Son—Tim right?"

I nodded at him, still not entirely sure what was going on or maybe not willing to acknowledge the truth.

"I think it would be best if you left here right now."

"What's going on?" I asked him with dread.

"Danielle's dead," he said bluntly. Next thing I realized I was looking up at the face of an EMT. And pushing the nasty smelling salts away from my face.

"Did we win?" I asked him.

"He's fine," The EMT said standing back up.

The cop came back and helped me sit up. He sat down next to me on the curb.

"Are you sure you've got the right girl?" I asked.

He nodded, his eyes full of kindness and sadness. "She didn't say what you did but she hung herself because of it."

I sobbed until my soul seemed wrung out.

"I hope you choke on it!" Mr. Hoegler said as the other cop moved him inside his house.

I never got the cop's name but he sat with me the whole time, until I felt my head was going to split.

"Did you learn anything here, son?" The cop asked with concern.

I nodded and I had. Never fall in love. I killed Donna Sorji's two Yorkshire Terriers, poisoned them with arsenic. I didn't care that they had nothing to do with the whole thing or that they were really her parents' dogs, I needed to strike out against her and it was either them or her. It was not long after that she became one of those homeschooled kids, my growling menacing looks at her more than likely sped the process up.

***

"You haven't aged at all," I told the girl in the back of that SUV. Higher reasoning wise I absolutely knew this wasn't Danielle, but that part of me was run completely over by the tide of feelings I had suppressed all these years. I retracted myself from the car, my need to feed momentarily forgotten. The dad let out a large wincing gush of air as I stepped on his stomach. I kicked him out of my way. My higher self knew that the illusion would be shattered once I opened up the rear door and got a closer look, but if anything it only reaffirmed my initial belief. She was beautiful and she even had that slightly lopsided smile that I had come to love.

"I knew they were lying!" I said as I gently picked her up from the seat. "Your father just didn't want me going out with you," I picked her up and cradled her in my arms. "You're so cold, Danielle," I said hugging her tight so that she could garner some of my body heat, although looking back that was probably a lesson in futility considering I was undead.

I kicked open the side garage door and into the day I went with Danielle in my arms, she didn't stir and she was as pale as a winter moon, but I knew she wasn't dead because of the way she was attracting zombies.

Fuck the pain. 'Hugh tell them to fuck off!' I screamed. No response and the zombies were closing in. "I will not lose you twice," I shouted, as I began to run, a full contingent of zombies in tow. I had put a fair amount of distance between us when my right leg stopped moving. 'What the hell! Hugh I need that!' I demanded.

Hugh was screaming some sort of high pitched cry, it sounded like torturous pain, a wailing cat being dragged upside down across glass. 'No... eat... dead!' he screamed. 'Other Hugh!'

'What does that mean? But I got it, even an offensive lineman can figure some shit out. I had eaten a dead infected human and now another virus or whatever the hell Hugh was, was now vying for control of this body and by my dead dragging right leg I could figure that my Hugh was losing.

I was still ahead of the horde but now I wasn't making anymore distance and unless Hugh rallied and began to win there was a very good chance I was going to lose function of another limb soon. I could not, would not fail Danielle again. I turned onto a side street hoping to lose a few of my denser pursuers, a white Ford pickup truck was parked up ahead at a convenience store the back was full of supplies that the people walking in and out of the store were filling it with.

I was close maybe fifty yards away when I made the turn and I could hear those people speak.

"Dad company!" A boy of about seventeen shouted looking over his shoulder. His gun was already at the ready.

Another man came out of the store, maybe somewhere in his mid forties, followed by a giant black man that made me look like Olive Oyl.

"Talbot, what the hell is that thing?" The black man asked his traveling companion.

"It's a clown. I hate clowns BT."

"Is there anything you *do* like?"

"I like you just fine."

"Aw, that's so sweet." A small female said as she came out of the store. "Is there something you need to tell me, Talbot?" she asked who I guessed was her significant other.

The man named Talbot pointed my way. I was going to shout but the invader worms/ Other Hugh had wrenched that control away also. Couldn't talk and dragging one leg behind me, might as well hang a placard over my head saying 'zombie'.

"Oh my God!" The woman cried. "Is he carrying someone?"

"I can smell him from here," the Talbot man gagged out.

"There's more of them Dad. A lot more." The boy yelled.

I had not fooled a single one of the zombies trailing me.

"Looks like he wants to eat that one all by himself," the giant BT said.

"Are you two going to help?" the woman asked.

'Yes, thank God. Please help me—us!' I thought.

I was within fifteen feet of the truck now and they weren't backing up but they weren't coming forward either.

"Mike, it's carrying a girl," BT said.

'IT!' I screamed indignantly in my head. 'Who the fuck is an IT, I'm TIMOTHY!'

Talbot's rifle was fixed squarely on my forehead. I could almost feel the laser etching into my skin. "I'm afraid the bullet will go through and hurt her."

"You sure she's not already dead?" the big black man asked him.

"Why don't you two debate about it a little longer?" the female said as she started to walk up towards me.

"Tracy what are you doing?" The man named Talbot asked her.

"I'm doing what it takes." The woman told her traveling companions, her resolve seemed less steeled as she approached.

She saw something in my one remaining eye which prodded her on. It could have been the spark of insanity, or tears of pleading for this to end, whatever it was she quickly closed the five feet that separated us and placed the muzzle of her pistol to my temple.

"Come on woman we have to go." Talbot shouted.

I didn't hear the shot and blissfully I didn't feel it as the bullet tore through my brain, all that you have read here are my last thoughts of the final split second I spent on this earth before eternal darkness and damnation clenched my soul forever in its cold cruel embrace. My name is Timothy and I am dead.

THE END

NECROPHOBIA
Jack Hamlyn

An ordinary summer's day.
The grass is green, the flowers are blooming. All is right with the world. Then the dead start rising. From cemetery and mortuary, funeral home and morgue, they flood into the streets until every town and city is infested with walking corpses, blank-eyed eating machines that exist to take down the living.

The world is a graveyard.

And when you have a family to protect, it's more than survival.

It's war!

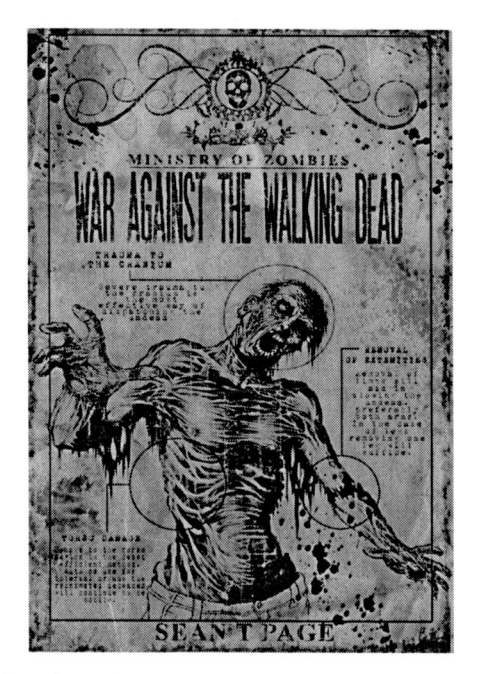

More than 63% of people now believe that there will be a global zombie apocalypse before 2050...
Employing real science and pioneering field work, War against the Walking Dead provides a complete blueprint for taking back your country from the rotting clutches of the dead after a zombie apocalypse.

* A glimpse inside the mind of the zombie using a team of top psychics - what do the walking dead think about? What lessons can we learn to help us defeat this pervading menace?
* Detailed guidelines on how to galvanise a band of scared survivors into a fighting force capable of defeating the zombies and dealing with emerging groups such as end of the world cults, raiders and even cannibals!
* Features insights from real zombie fighting organisations across the world, from America to the Philippines, Australia to China - the experts offer advice in every aspect of fighting the walking dead.

Packed with crucial zombie war information and advice, from how to build a city of the living in a land of the dead to tactics on how to use a survivor army to liberate your country from the zombies - War against the Walking Dead may be humanity's last chance.

Remember, dying is not an option!

WHITE FLAG OF THE DEAD
Joseph Talluto

**Book 1
Surrender of the Living.**

Millions died when the Enillo Virus swept the earth. Millions more were lost when the victims of the plague refused to stay dead, instead rising to slay and feed on those left alive. For survivors like John Talon and his son Jake, they are faced with a choice: Do they submit to the dead, raising the white flag of surrender? Or do they find the will to fight, to try and hang on to the last shreds or humanity?

Surrender of the Living is the first high octane installment in the White Flag of the Dead series.

RESURRECTION
By Tim Curran

The rain is falling and the dead are rising. It began at an ultra-secret government laboratory. Experiments in limb regeneration- an unspeakable union of Medieval alchemy and cutting edge genetics result in the very germ of horror itself: a gene trigger that will reanimate dead tissue...any dead tissue. Now it's loose. It's gone viral. It's in the rain. And the rain has not stopped falling for weeks. As the country floods and corpses float in the streets, as cities are submerged, the evil dead are rising. And they are hungry.

"I REALLY love this book...Curran is a wonderful storyteller who really should be unleashed upon the general horror reading public sooner rather than later." – *DREAD CENTRAL*

Dead Bait

"If you don't already suffer from bathophobia and/or ichthyophobia, you probably will after reading this amazingly wonderful horrific collection of short stories about what lurks beneath the waters of the world" – *DREAD CENTRAL*

A husband hell-bent on revenge hunts a Wereshark...A Russian mail order bride with a fishy secret...Crabs with a collective consciousness...A vampire who transforms into a Candiru...Zombie piranha...Bait that will have you crawling out of your skin and more. Drawing on horror, humor with a helping of dark fantasy and a touch of deviance, these 19 contemporary stories pay homage to the monsters that lurk in the murky waters of our imaginations. ***If you thought it was safe to go back in the water...Think Again!***

"Severed Press has the cojones to publish THE most outrageous, nasty and downright wonderfully disgusting horror that I've seen in quite a while." – *DREAD CENTRAL*

ZOMBIE ZOOLOGY
Unnatural History:

Severed Press has assembled a truly original anthology of never before published stories of living dead beasts. Inside you will find tales of prehistoric creatures rising from the Bog, a survivalist taking on a troop of rotting baboons, a NASA experiment going Ape, A hunter going a Moose too far and many more undead creatures from Hell. The crawling, buzzing, flying abominations of mother nature have risen and they are hungry.

"Clever and engaging a reanimated rarity"
FANGORIA

"I loved this very unique anthology and highly recommend it"
Monster Librarian

BIOHAZARD
Tim Curran

The day after tomorrow: Nuclear fallout. Mutations. Deadly pandemics. Corpse wagons. Body pits. Empty cities. The human race trembling on the edge of extinction. Only the desperate survive. One of them is Rick Nash. But there is a price for survival: communion with a ravenous evil born from the furnace of radioactive waste. It demands sacrifice. Only it can keep Nash one step ahead of the nightmare that stalks him-a sentient, seething plague-entity that stalks its chosen prey: the last of the human race. To accept it is a living death. To defy it, a hell beyond imagining

"kick back and enjoy some the most violent and genuinely scary apocalyptic horror written by one of the finest dark fiction authors plying his trade today" HORRORWORLD

www.severedpress.com